The Tracks

Kendra Smith

Contents

Stolen Moments

R iley's POV

I slowly sat up on the edge of the bed the sheets falling around me. My feet brushed the carpet as my heart dropped to my toes. I couldn't look back over my shoulder at the sleeping man behind me or I wouldn't be able to leave. I went to stand up as I felt the bed shift behind me. Closing my eyes, I sighed as a pair of arms slipped around my waist tugging me back against a warm chest. A shiver slipped down my spine as he brushed a soft kiss across the top of my tan shoulder.

"You could always stay," he murmured kissing a slow path to the curve of my neck grazing it with his teeth. I threaded my fingers with his big hands wishing I could. "Run away with me and don't look back."

"You know I can't B," I whispered quietly as I turned my head brushing my lips along his. I pulled away before he could deepen it. "No matter how much I want to, I can't. Would be hell to pay and you know it."

"Dammit Riles," Brantley grumbled dropping his arms from around me and stretching back out on the wrecked bed as I pushed to my feet gathering my clothes to tug on. "I don't get why you won't divorce his ass."

"I've tried," I snapped glaring at him tugging my black lace underwear on before donning the matching bra. I whirled around my honey blonde hair flying as tears glittered in my grey eyes. "You know I have. You need to give me up B. I've tried to tell you to for years and we are still doing the same song and dance. You deserve to have the life and family you have always wanted. Quit letting me hold you back."

"I want that with you Riley," he said with a sigh glaring at me propping up on his elbows. Those intense green eyes that always made me melt following my every move. I slipped into the yoga pants I'd had on and searched around for my tank top that was flung over the chair in the corner. "I told you years ago I wasn't giving up baby girl and I'm not. I will take you anyway I can get you."

"So secret meetings in hotel rooms throughout the country is the way to go," I argued pulling my tank top on. I settled my hands on my narrow hips as I met his eyes in challenge. "Slipping in to see you when I go to Mama's. PJ is the only one who knows that you aren't on that bus right now headed to the next tour stop. He knows that you came to see me. What we have is so fucking unhealthy on so many levels it's not even funny. It's time to give me up B."

"No," he growled glaring at me. I threw my hands up in a huff as I searched for my shoes. I needed to get back to my own room, get my stuff and get back on a plane to Atlanta. "Riles.....look at me please."

"No," I said shaking my head as I twisted my hair up into a messy bun.

"Please," he said again gently and I vehemently shook my head as tears welled in my eyes. I turned my back to him busying myself looking for my shoes when a moment later I felt heat at my back and I sighed. "Whatever you need I'll help Riley. Say the damn word. He can threaten and bluster all he wants. I don't give a damn that it's his ring on your hand or his last name, you are mine. Have been since we were five years old."

"It's not that simple B," I sighed leaning my head back against his chest closing my eyes. "If it were I would have been gone. I can't keep dragging you down. Please, I am begging you. Find someone else and settle down. Forget all about me."

"I've told you a hundred times before and I will again Riley Nicole," Brantley whispered in my ear making me shiver settling those big hands on my shoulders. "I'm not going anywhere. Swear to all that is holy if you help our mama's to try and set me up again, you will need a pillow to sit on the next time I see you."

"Well as your best friend," I muttered ducking out of his arms and slipping my shoes on. I gave him a smirk that earned me a snarl as he turned to tug his jeans on. "They value my opinion."

"The only damn woman I want is you," Brantley grumbled rolling his eyes at me. "My mama has suspected something has still been going on with us for years. Yours, bless her, has still been in the dark. Jackson has her so convinced he's this awesome guy. Swear, if I ever find another bruise on you again Riles, he's a dead man."

"It makes her happy so don't lose your temper B," I sighed looking for my phone. "Was Daddy's last good memory of me okay. Listen, I've got to go. I'll miss my flight back if I don't." I grabbed my phone off the nightstand and hurried to the door. I had to get out of here. I couldn't have this same argument for the millionth time. My hand was on the door knob to open it when a big, ringed hand covered mine the other one slapping the wood of the door near my head. "I've got to go B."

"I know," he murmured into my hair with a sigh. "See you this week?"

"Yea," I whispered. "I told Mama I would be coming by. You know her and Ms. Becky are thick as thieves."

"Be safe please," Brantley said turning me around to face him reaching up to stroke a thumb across my cheek. He lowered his head brushing his lips against mine softly before taking a step back. "Let me know when you land okay."

"I will," I said giving him a quick smile and turning around to open the door. "Love you B."

"Love you too Riles," I heard replied as I hurried out the door and down the hall.

An hour later I was boarding my flight back to Atlanta. I settled into my window seat looking out at the clouds feeling my eyes well with tears. My life would be so much simpler if had never said yes. Which led to me saying I do. My life was supposed to be different and now I did my best to hide behind my camera lens as much as I could. Traveling the world, photo after photo, and it was the stolen moments of my life that were hidden from the camera that truly made me smile. Later that night I wearily pulled in the driveway of the cookie cutter two story brick mini mansion we owned in Alpharetta.

I had conceded to this house just because it was closer to Jefferson and my mom. I hit the button on my visor to open the garage and noted that Jackson's BMW wasn't inside. Rolling my eyes, I should have known. I was out of town. He must be shacked up with the latest secretary. Climbing out, I pulled my luggage out slinging my camera bag over my shoulder. I would go through the photos tomorrow. I trudged into the cool, quiet house with a weary sigh as I walked up the stairs heading to my room at the end of the hall. I'd given up any pretense of this marriage working a couple years ago and moved into another room.

Walking into my room, I dropped my bags down and headed into the bathroom to grab a quick shower. Less than ten minutes later I drug my tired body to the bed running a comb through my hair after slipping on an old football jersey of Brantley's. I slipped under the covers with a sigh as my eyes welled with tears. Leaving him each time got harder, but I wasn't free to give either of us what we wanted. What killed me is I knew he blamed himself for some of this. I'd giving anything to go back to before it all went to hell. Only upside to this was no matter how twisted things may be, I hadn't lost my best friend. I needed him as much as he needed me. I'd always loved him no matter what. I drifted off to sleep focusing on the good memories I had and clung to them.

Heading Home

R iley's POV

    I took the exit heading to the house rubbing my hand over neck to ease some of the tension there. I'd wound up falling asleep in the loft of my studio the last few nights. Only one phone call from Jackson to find out if I was even back in town. Yea, some marriage we had. He had just graduated law school when I met him back in 2010. I had been taking every photography job I could land with plans of opening my own studio while making trips back and forth to the hospital with Daddy slowly going downhill. Between Daddy's cancer spreading, Mama going out of her mind with worry, and Brantley hell bent on the bottle at the time, I had been stretched thin. Jackson had been sweet, attentive, and handsome.

He'd come in and literally swept me off my feet at the time. I had needed the support at the time since I had only been getting it sparingly. He had listened to me when I had cried worried about my daddy and my best friend, made sure I got rest and sleep. Deep down, I knew he wasn't who I wanted by my side through all of it, but I was thankful for what I had. Brantley and I had drifted apart for the first time in a long time since we had split up after high school. He'd met Amber a few years after and had been back and forth with her for a while until she hadn't been able to stand the drinking either.

Sometimes I wished I had a time machine, that I had picked up on just what a dickhead Jackson could be beforehand. He'd charmed my parents in record time after meeting them at first. Looking back now, I guess it worked because all three of us had been vulnerable. Daddy had seen me happy and it had been his dying wish for me to stay that way. Part of the reason I was still in the situation I was in years later. Pulling into the driveway, I parked my SUV and climbed out. I needed to get my bag and head to Mama's. I had promised her I would come by for a few days since I'd been out of town. I noticed Jackson's car parked as well making me sigh. Unlocking the front door, I headed inside, pausing when I heard my name being called from the kitchen. I quietly groaned under my breath then walked into the room.

Jackson was sitting on a barstool at the marble countertop eating a salad with his tie tossed over his shoulder. I saw the matching grey Armani suit jacket draped over the chair behind him. He raised a dark eyebrow at me as I walked in. Those cold blue eyes watching me closely. Jackson Deveraux was devastatingly handsome, but the asshole underneath the Southern charm and polish reared his head more than often now. While he had never come right out and hit me, he had from time to time gripped my wrist or arms tight enough to leave fingerprint bruises.

Last time he had, it had taken PJ and I both twenty minutes to calm Brantley down when he saw them. I'd tried to hide it. But the damn man knew me better than anyone, so he'd known something was wrong. I walked closer leaning my hip against the counter as Jackson and I stared each other down. The neatly cropped black hair, tan skin, tall, trim body that once drove me wild for a brief time. Now, I couldn't stand to be closer to him than I had to. Jackson took another bite of salad chewing thoughtfully as he looked at me before pasting a serene smile on his full lips.

"How was your trip sweetheart?" Jackson inquired. I could see the calculation in his blue eyes as I shook my head.

"It was fine," I answered between clenched teeth drumming a nail on the countertop.

"Always find it funny that your shoots can sometimes be timed around tour stops," Jackson said laying his fork down with a humorless chuckle. I glared at him with as much venom as I could muster. Always the same song and dance.

"That's a pure coincidence and you know it Jax," I snapped back rolling my eyes. "For the last time, back off that topic."

"Ahhh," Jackson said with an evil smile. "You can't tell me that you haven't still be seeing him. You come home smiling. And not that fake one you past one for appearances."

"Like I overlook the string of secretaries," I snarled crossing my arms over my chest. He tried to feign shock at my words. "What, didn't realize I knew about them? Maybe I do see Brantley still. We are old friends, he's still remained my best friend all these years. Our moms are super close."

"Friends....." Jackson drawled getting up to put his plate in the sink. A second later he braced his hands on either side of me on the counter leaning in my ear. "Hmmm... we will go with that. Ever wonder why Jana didn't work? God, that was a hot piece of ass let me tell you. Then Amber walks away again, the supposed love of his life. I know I do.

"Jana didn't work because she was a bitch," I snapped as he pressed closer to me making me shiver and not in a good way. "Just used him as a stepping stone to further her career. Amber couldn't handle the spotlight."

"Can convince me of that all you want," Jackson snarled lowly in my ear. "But you are the reason neither of them worked. Still hung up on you after all these years. But if you want to keep this charade up that's fine with me."

"Then why won't you just give me what I want," I said closing my eyes as tears of frustration welled in them. "Why the hell won't you give me the divorce I want? Jax, you don't love me and I don't love you."

"Because honey," Jackson said with a wide grin rubbing his hands over my shoulders. "My firm frowns on divorced partners so you are an asset to me. They love you. So no, I'm not giving you up."

"You won't give me up because your jealous of him," I growled pushing Jackson back and ducking under his arm. "Always have been since you figured out our history. Keeping me tied to you is your way of one uping him. Just give me up Jax!"

"NO!" he roared slapping his hands onto the counter with a loud thud making me jump. His eyes narrowed dangerously as he looked at me. "You are my wife! Don't fucking forget it. You may be spreading your legs for him, but it's still my ring on your finger and my last name you carry. Don't fucking forget it!"

"Like you let me!" I yelled back before turning on my foot and jogging up the stairs to grab the bag I'd left packed. I stalked back down the stairs to see Jackson slipping his suit jacket on and staring me down.

"Where are you headed?" he inquired like he gave a damn. He'd spend time at the apartment he thought I didn't know about near the law firm office. No doubt with his latest bed partner. I had heard rumor one of the senior partners new, young, second wife had caught his eye.

"To Mama's" I replied haughtily daring him to say a word. He smirked then nodded.

"Well be sure to send my regards dear," he drawled tapping his chin with a smug look. "I'm sure you'll be spending a little time in Maysville while you are there."

"Fuck off Jax," I growled before storming out the door and getting on the road. I pounded the wheel in frustration as I got on the road.

An hour later I pulled into Mama's driveway with a sigh. I slipped my sunglasses off and pushed my blonde hair out of my face as I grabbed my bag and headed up the steps of my childhood home. Always felt bittersweet coming home and Daddy not being here. I opened the front door and called out for Mama only to be met with silence. Knowing her, I made my way out to the back deck she had added a few years ago and found her and Ms. Becky sitting at the outdoor table with a plate of cookies and a pitcher of lemonade between them. They were cackling like a pair of loons and I couldn't help but smile.

"I swear," I called out as I made my way closer. "You two always find something to gossip about."

"Oh hush!" Mama called out as Ms. Becky started laughing. She gave a wink before picking up her phone typing out a text. I didn't even have to ask. I knew what it said. More than likely was your girl's home too. Mama jumped up giving me a big hug and I inhaled her familiar vanilla scent letting it sooth my nerves. She pulled back framing my face with her hands. "Missed you honey."

"Missed you too Mama," I said with a smile giving Ms. Becky a hug before sitting down. Her phone chimed beside her and she grinned as I shook my head.

"Oh honey," Mama said jumping up her blonde ponytail bouncing as she started towards the house. "I made those teacakes you love sweetie. Jackson going to come in later?"

"No mam," I said with a forced smile. "Got a big case he's working on. Barely had time to see me when I got back the other day."

"That boy works too hard," Mama said shaking her head as she disappeared in the house. I turned my head seeing Ms. Becky's knowing look. She reached over laying a hand over mine as I took a sip of the lemonade. She had suspected something had still be going on between me and Brantley just never said anything.

"You okay sweetheart?" she asked quietly. I turned my head giving her a fake smile nodding my head.

"Yes mam," I answered with false cheeriness. I shrank back a little at the piercing look that I normally got from Brantley and sighed. "I am honestly."

"Mhmm..." Ms. Becky said patting my hand with a sigh. She didn't say anymore since Mama came back out with the tea cakes with a wide smile handing me the plate. I picked one up taking a bite. I almost choked on it as I heard the familiar rumble of a motorcycle pull into the driveway next door. I couldn't help my heartbeat speeding up a little at the sound. Ms. Becky smiled around her glass as she took a sip and Mama started telling me about the latest gossip from town. A minute later the gate for the backyard open revealing Brantley as he strode through. I discreetly bit my lip as I took in the sight of the backwards black hat, ripped jeans, and cut off Bulldogs t-shirt showing off those arms and ink. His eyes covered by dark glasses, but I could feel them studying me as he approached us with a wide grin across his lip.

"Brantley son, when did you get home?" Mama asked with a wide smile.

"Yesterday," Brantley rumbled giving her a hug. "How have you been Ms. Lainey?"

"Good honey," Mama said patting his arm. "Doing good."

"Hey angel," he murmured leaning down giving Ms. Becky a big hug before turning to me. He leaned down brushing a soft kiss on the top of my head before settling into the chair beside me stretching his long legs out. "Doing okay Riles?"

"Yea B," I said giving him a smile. I jumped a little when I felt warm hand settle over my bare knee where my shorts ended, catching a slight smirk out of the corner of my eye. Damn man was impossible sometimes.

"Riley honey," Mama said turning her scrutinizing look on me. Shit, here we go. "When you are you and Jackson going to give me some grandkids?"

"Mama....." I groaned feeling Brantley's grip tighten on my knee before stroking his thumb slowly across my skin. "We've talked about this. As much as I travel its just not a good idea."

"Then cut back on traveling," Mama said waving a hand at me. Yea..um m..no. My job was my escape. "Jackson makes more than enough for you to stay at home. Let photography just be your hobby while the kids are young."

"Mama," I murmured feeling my shoulders stiffen. Lord, I loved her to pieces but sometimes I wanted to go off on her with how much of a saint she thought Jackson was. "Jackson doesn't think it's a good time either right now so just drop it." I lowered my voice muttering to myself. "Have to actually be sleeping with each other first."

Brantley covered his chuckle up with a quiet cough as I glared over at him. I heard a huff from Mama and bit the inside of my cheek to keep a sigh in.

"One of these days y'all will realize you aren't getting any younger," Mama grumbled.

"We will see," I said rolling my eyes. "Not like you can make me Mama."

"Well I can hope can't I?" Mama said cocking an eyebrow at me. Then she looked over at Ms. Becky. " I swear Becky, between our three kids dragging their heels we are gonna be a pair of old maids.

"Speak for yourself Lainey," Ms. Becky said with a snort. "I have a man. Keeps me young let me tell you."

"Maammmmaaa...." Brantley groaned as I started to laugh. She turned her head narrowing her eyes at him. "Can we please not go there?"

"Why not son?" Ms. Becky inquired. "I have heard enough about your sex life and Kolby's enough over the years to last me a lifetime. Justice served as far as I'm concerned."

I lost it laughing then. She gave me a pointed look as I heard a quiet growl slip past Brantley's lips. That was exactly how she knew we still had something going on. She had walked in on us a couple years ago not knowing I was there. Of course, we had gotten read the riot act because I was married. After I explained things to her a little more she frowned about it a little less. I knew she was worried about both of us getting burned in the end. My only problem was, I still loved Brantley more than anything. A piece of paper and changing my name hadn't changed it like I thought it would.

"Quit encouraging her Riles," Brantley sighed as the rest of us laughed. I choked on the sip of lemonade I was taking as his big hand slid further up my leg but never took his eyes off his Mama. "Okay over there?"

"Fine," I said through clenched teeth kicking his ankle hard enough to make him wince as I pushed to my feet. "On that note, Mama, I am out. I promised a certain princess a tea party and make overs when I got in."

"Tinsley sure has missed you," Ms. Becky said with a grin. I leaned over giving Mama a hug as I heard Brantley speak behind me.

"Want me to tag along?" he asked going to stand up.

"Unless you want our goddaughter to try and put pink lipstick on you again," I said with a snicker as he shuddered. "I would sit this one out outlaw."

"Yea," he said with a chuckle. "I think I will stay out of it. Last time she did that, Ashley tried her damnedest to put it on Instagram. I'll swing by and see her tomorrow."

"Alright," I said with a laugh heading to the back door. "Mama don't wait up. You know how Ashley and I get when we get together."

"Lord help Eli," I heard my Mama call after me making me laugh.

Drunken Thoughts

B rantley's POV

I glanced down at the time on my phone seeing it was after midnight and sighed. Out of the corner of my eye I noticed the headlights pulling up the drive and pushed to my bare feet padding to the front door swinging it open. I leaned against the door frame watching Eli climb out of his truck shaking his head before opening the back door. I couldn't help but chuckle as he slammed the door and walked around the back of his truck with a giggling Riley tossed over his shoulder. Ashley rolled the passenger window down hanging out to wave at her. If her goofy ass leaned any further out she would fall out of the truck.

I rubbed a hand over my beard shaking my head as Eli got closer muttering under his breath. I laughed when I noticed Riley had on a bright pink pair of fuzzy pajama pants and what looked like a BG Nation t-shirt. Sure sign right there that the girls were getting drunk if they already had their pj's on. Claimed they learned it was easier years ago so they were comfy and ready to crash. They'd had the entire MC laughing one night when we were younger at them shooting tequila in their pajamas. Eli stopped in front of me rolling his eyes as I laughed.

"I take it they got wine locked huh?" I chuckled. Riley swiveled her head around to give me a toothy drunken grin before her hair fell in her face. She tried to huff blowing it out the way with no luck. She smacked Eli in the middle of his back for bouncing her.

"Lord did they," Eli said with a sigh sliding Riley off his shoulder dodging a kick as he passed her over. "They killed a couple bottles of wine and cleaned the entire house out of chocolate. They were bribing Kolby to go get them some more when I cut them off. She's gonna have a hell of a headache in the morning." I nodded as I scooped her up in my arms. Riley's arms automatically wrapping around my neck as she buried her face in my shoulder with a sigh. Eli gave me a knowing look. "I'll be honest BG, from what little I overheard, she needed tonight."

"Yea," I murmured tightening my hold on her. Times like this I wished I could hold her and never let go. Seeing her at the end of last week had been the first time in a month we'd been able to find the time. It hurt not being able to see Riley how and when I wanted to. "I know. Thanks bro."

"See you later B," Eli called out as he headed back out to his truck. I turned heading into the house kicking the door closed with my foot before walking to the stairs. My foot slipped on the first step when I felt a warm pair of lips travel up the side of my neck making me groan.

"Riles....." I ground out through clenched teeth locking my knees as she swirled her tongue over my pulse.

"Hmmm...." she muttered grazing her teeth on the underside of my jaw. I paused at the top of the stairs looking down at her.

"Better quit before you get something started," I muttered as she gave me a drunken wink.

"That's the plan," Riley chimed back sassily with a slight slur. I growled low in my throat as I stalked into my room sitting her slowly down on her feet. I hated to break it to her, that wasn't happening tonight. I knew from experience it wouldn't be long before she crashed. I bit the inside of my cheek as Riley stepped forward pressing against me dragging a finger down my chest tracing over my tattoos before stopping at the edge of my shorts. She pulled at the waistband giving me a wide smile. "Think these need to go B."

"No, no they don't Riles," I muttered closing my eyes when she leaned forward pressing a soft kiss to the middle of my chest before sliding her hand down further. I grabbed her hand entwining her fingers with mine. I opened my eyes to look down at her as she looked up at me poking her bottom lip out and shaking her blonde hair out of her face. Those beautiful gray eyes full of need. "Don't pout at me."

"You're being a stubborn ass," Riley grumbled glaring at me trying to pull her hand free. "God, I need you. I can clearly tell you want me as much as I want you."

"Because baby," I whispered leaning down to brush my lips over hers. "You are drunk and can barely see straight as it is." Riley lifted her head glaring at me dangerously. Oh boy, a temper tantrum could be coming. Damn woman was all sass on a good day. I slid my hand around smacking her pajama clad bottom sharply one time making her gasp. "Don't you give me that look woman. I always want you, you know that."

"Me being drunk used to never stop you," Riley grumbled pushing a hand into my chest making me take a step back. My jaw clenched when she reached down grasping the ends of her t-shirt slowly tugging it over her head revealing all that warm, smooth, tan skin. I got a naughty grin as the shirt cleared her head and she shook out her soft blonde hair. I couldn't help but follow her hand with my eyes as she licked her lips and reached behind her to unhook the red lace bra she was wearing. I did my damnedest to ignore the flash of the diamond on her finger in the low light. It hurt knowing it wasn't my ring she was wearing.

My eyes trailed down her body to the curve of her hip that was exposed from her low riding pants. There in cursive black ink was one word, BOSS surrounded with wings like the ones on my right side. I grinned thinking about her surprising me with it right after she turned eighteen. Back when we were young and dumb enough to think we could have it all. From what she had told me, Jackson bought her story that it was a funny dare from Ashley on senior trip. Riley put her hands on those curved hips glaring at me and those full breasts bounce. I swallowed deeply as she arched her eyebrow at me. "I can remember us getting quite creative back in the day."

"We are both a lot older now Riles," I grumbled through clenched teeth trying to keep myself in control. I was met with an eye roll. Riley flipped me off before hooking her thumbs in the waist of her pajama pants slipping them down her toned legs leaving her standing in front of me in just a scrap of red lace she called underwear. I looked at the ceiling praying for patience. "Riley....."

"But dammit B!" she snapped swaying as she tried to stalk over to me. I grabbed her elbow to keep her from tumbling over. "I need you. God do I. IIII....need to feel like a damn woman. One that a man finds sexy and keep his hands off of. That's always been you and here you are standing in front of me telling me no."

"Ok, that's it," I grumbled tugging Riley gently along with me and grabbing her shirt off the bed. I slipped it over her head then pushed her back on the bed before climbing in beside her. I nudged her with my hip making her scoot to the middle before rolling over bracing my hands on either side of her head. Her breath hitched as I hovered over her, lifting my hand to brush the hair away from her face. It would be so easy to just slip those lace panties to the side and slip into her giving her what we both craved.

I ached with the thought and willed myself to calm down. What I get for trying to be a gentleman. "You are beautiful, and sexy. Dammit Riles, you are everything I could ever want or need." I leaned down kissing her slowly taking my time earning me a whimper from deep in her throat. I broke the kiss laying my head against hers. "Please don't forget that."

"Then show me," Riley pleaded wrapping her legs around me waist pulling me closer. "We never know when we will get the chance to be together. This may be the last time for a while. I never know when I can slip away. God, please B. I need you to remind me of who I am. Not who I am expected to be."

"You......are......mine," I whispered pressing my lips to hers with each word as I stared in her eyes. The tears I saw gathering there made my heart ache. Riley sniffled as she lifted her small hand to cup the side of my face stroking her thumb there with a sigh. "That's who you are."

"But I'm not," she murmured as the tears slipped down her cheeks. "No matter how much I want to be, I'm not. He refuses to let me go. I don't love him and I want out. Brantley, I'm so damn miserable and then Mama just had to go and bring up kids today. You know what a sore subject that is for me and she doesn't even know."

"I don't care what a fucking piece of paper says Riley," I growled low in my throat making her eyes widen. I couldn't help it. The tears were killing me. Fuck, I'd been lost that day a few years ago she had called me out of the blue bawling her eyes out. "You are mine because I've got the one thing he doesn't and that's your heart baby. You know that all you have to do is say the word and I will bring the whole damn state down on his head until he does sign those damn papers."

"And the publicity from that would ruin you!" Riley whimpered shaking her head at me as the tears fell. Fuck Eli was right, she was due for a breakdown. I gently wiped at her cheek with the back of my hand. "I know you don't care and you are all about what you see is what you get. Most people expect that out of you Brantley, but you and I both know that there is still a certain morale backbone to country music. And the way Jackson would spin it, it would be horrible. It's my fight. Please let me handle it. You can't fight every battle for me anymore. It's probably going to be best that when I go back, I keep my distance for a little while."

"Fuck that Riley!" I snapped then sighed as she started to cry harder. I rolled to my side pulling her close wrapping my arms around her. Riley tucked her head under my chin and I closed my eyes when I felt the tears hit my chest. "I don't give a shit you know that. Hell, I'll run the farm the rest of my life. I don't give a damn if I ever played another song again as long as you are free to be with me. I fucked up years ago not being there for you when I should have. Dammit, I'm not doing it again. Let me handle it please."

"No," she whispered shaking her head. "I can't let my mistake ruin you and your career. It means the world to you B. Whether you know it or not, if you couldn't play music anymore it would kill a part of your soul. Eventually, you would end up hating me since I would be the cause. I couldn't bear that."

"Riles," I sighed throwing my head back against the pillow. "It's not your fault. If I had stepped up then to be the man you needed me to be instead of hiding in the bottle, Jackson wouldn't be in the picture. Baby, I am so sorry for that. I wish I could go back and change it. Kills me that Mike's last memories of me were of a drunken jackass who made his baby girl cry. You know, Jackson wouldn't let me in to see him to say goodbye. Told me that it would upset you." Riley sucked in a sob clinging to me a little tighter. I pulled her tighter to me kissing the top of her head stroking a hand up and down her back. "Let's table this talk for the night okay baby. Not the best talk to have when one of us is drunk."

"Told me a long time ago that drunk words are sober thoughts," Riley mumbled with a sigh her soft lips brushing along my skin.

"I know," I whispered softly as her breathing started to level out as her tears subsided. "I love you Riley Nicole."

"Forever and always Brantley Keith," Rileymumbled back sleepily clinging to me as she finally fell asleep. I held her alittle tighter feeling like I was losing her all over again. I had my wholeworld in my arms and she was tying my hands on trying to step in and take her heartache away.

Flashback: Life Changing News: Part I

June 2015

Riley's POV

I tapped my nails on my knee as Jackson leaned against the wall of the exam room tapping away on his phone. I narrowed my eyes at the half smile on his face as he read something wondering what he could be happy about. I was a nervous wreck awaiting these results. About a year ago, Ashley had called me to tell me that Amber was back. That she had heard she had plans to make the effort to get in touch with Brantley. I hung up the phone and had taken a good hard look at my life. For about a year after Jana was out of the picture, we had been sneaking around when we could to see each other. Still kept up the basis we were best friends, which wasn't a lie, we were.

But I was holding him back from living his life. I wasn't free to give him the life and family he deserved, she was. So when he called to tell me she'd contacted him, I sucked it up and wholeheartedly encouraged him to see her. I had then resolved myself to doing what I could to make my marriage work. I'd thought I was in love with Jackson in the beginning maybe I could be again. One of us deserved a happily ever after. I had sat him down and had a long serious talk with him. I had suspected about him having an affair just never had proof. I discussed the subject of kids and we had agreed to try.

Won't say it had been hearts and flowers the last few months, but it had been okay for a little while. Jackson had even seemed to be making an effort at first. B had gotten back with Amber and I was happy for him even if it killed me a little. I'd always felt like she had replaced me even in the beginning. I avoided going home when I could and put a little more time in traveling. Jackson went with me a few times at first then his cases started piling up. So here we were months later and month after month of no luck in getting pregnant. The door swung open pulling me from my thoughts as Dr. Jacobs walked in shutting the door behind him. He had grown up with Jackson and when we first started talking about trying Jackson had wanted me to see him. Apparently, there was this new vitamin that had hit the market that helped increase our chances. Yea.... no such luck for me. I mean I know I was getting older but damn, I wasn't over the hill by any means.

"Ah Mrs. Deveraux honey how are you?" Dr. Jacobs said giving me a quick smile before extending a hand out to Jackson. "Jackson hey man. Still on for golf tomorrow?"

"You know it," Jackson said with a wink before sliding his phone into his suit pocket. Here it was I was on pins and needles about my reproductive future and these two asshats were worried about golf! Dr. Jacobs turned his head towards me giving me a look before clearing his throat and opening the folder in his hand. He looked over at Jackson quickly. "Well Doc, how's my beautiful bride?"

"I'm afraid I have some bad news Mrs. Deveraux," Dr. Jacobs said pulling up his stool. I felt my heart sink to my toes as my skin paled. One would think my husband would be rushing to my side from the look of fear on my face. But no, he remained propped against the wall and indiscreetly glancing at his watch.

"Riley, please," I murmured clasping my hands together reaching down for every ounce of strength I had.

"Riley," Dr. Jacobs said quietly. "I'm afraid the results aren't good. There is a lot of scarring and scar tissue on your cervix and fallopian tubes. I know you said you had regular check ups but it must be something your doctor didn't catch. I must say, I'm surprised you haven't had any pain."

"Well darling you do have those pain pills you take," Jackson said nonchalantly.

"For when I have a bad migraine," I snapped through clenched teeth trying to reign in my temper when I was shot a disapproving look. Of course, be the good little wife in front of the right people Riley. "Those are only on an as needed basis Doctor. So what are you trying to tell me?"

"We've tested both of you thoroughly," Dr. Jacobs said adjusting his glasses. I swear the man looked like a southern country club version of Peter Parker. "Jax here is in perfect health. But with your issues, I have to say, I don't see any chances at all of you conceiving. If you were to, wouldn't be possible for you to carry the fetus to term. I am very sorry."

"Oh my god," I whispered covering my mouth with my hand as tears welled up in my eyes. Dr. Jacobs gave me a sympathetic smile. I glanced over at Jackson who calmly slid his hands into his slack pockets studying me. I felt my blood boil at the shrug of his shoulders and narrowed my eyes.

"Well...um.... I will just give you both a few minutes alone," Dr. Jacobs said before hopping up and scurrying out the door. It clicked closed behind him. Jackson stepped closer to me as the tears slipped down my cheeks unchecked. I wanted a family of my own so damn bad and my last shot at happiness just went up in a puff of smoke.

"Now, now dear, dry your eyes," Jackson said patting my arm as he stood in front of me and sighed. "Look at it this way sweetheart, I mean, did we truly have time for a child with how much we both work? I can't cut back and I doubt you really want to. Maybe it is for the best."

"For the best!" I snapped glaring at him choking back a sob. "For the best that I am incapable of doing the one thing a woman is made for! For the best that all my friends are on their second or third child and I can't even have one!" I raised my hand to slap him as tears fell harder only to be stopped with an iron grip around my wrist the long fingers digging in hard making me whimper. "Let me go Jax."

"When you calm down Riley," Jackson growled looming over me shaking my arm slightly making me wince in pain as he narrowed those cold blue eyes making my heart pound. "You are just going to have to accept this and move on. Now, dry you eyes and fix your face. I have to head back to the office and catch up on the appointments I missed from being here. You know how busy I am. Don't forget that we have dinner with a couple of the senior partners tonight at seven. Please don't be late."

"I'm sitting this one out Jax," I muttered yanking my arm away and cradling it to me. Fuck, that was going to be sore tomorrow. "Just make my excuses. Tell them I got called out of town for a shoot or I'm ill. I really don't care. Whatever excuse makes you look the best. I need some time to process this."

"Fine," Jackson said through clenched teeth giving me a curt nod. "Get it together so you don't embarrass me." With that he turned on his heel and stormed out of the room. I buried my face in my hands trying to get a grip on my emotions as my arm throbbed with my heartbeat. Taking a deep breath, I summoned up all the courage I could and slipped off the table to slip out of the room on shaky legs.

Knowing there was a back door, I ducked my head as I hurried past a group of nurses and slipped out into the parking lot. I dug my keys out of my purse. It took me two tries to unlock my SUV they were shaking so bad. I finally was able to unlock the door and slid into the driver's seat before my legs collapsed. I said a quick prayer before starting the vehicle and backing out of the parking slot and pointed my car towards home. Please, please just let me make it to my spot before I totally lost it.

Forty-five minutes later I was on the interstate, out of Atlanta and getting closer to my destination. I hadn't stopped crying the entire drive but had managed to make the drive mainly from memory and the grace of God. My wrist was throbbing as the skin was starting to bruise from Jackson's fingers. I glanced over at my phone in the cupholder near me and bit my lip debating with myself. I desperately wanted to dial the one number I hadn't in months. I mean we exchanged a text here and there but for the main part I'd kept my distance. When I couldn't stand it anymore, I snatched my phone up hitting the speed dial. It rang a few times and I almost broke down thinking I was going to be sent to voicemail when the line clicked.

"Riles?" Brantley asked sounding a little shocked I had actually called. I couldn't keep my sniffles in then. I tried to hold the wheel steady as I wiped at my eyes and tried to make words form. "Riley, honey what's the matter? I can tell you are crying. Where are you?"

"Bbbbb..." I stuttered taking a deep breath. "I hate to call, but I need you. Any way I can get you to meet me at our spot? Shit, you are probably on the road aren't you. Shit, I'm sorry. I shouldn't......"

"Riles," I heard growled in my ear making me stop. "I'll see you there. Twenty minutes good?"

"Yes," I whispered feeling slightly relieved.

"Alright be careful and I will see you soon," Brantley answered before hanging up the phone. I placed my phone back in the cupholder and gripped the steering wheel tightly in both hands mustering up the strength I needed to get where I was going.

Flashback: Life Changing News: Part II

B rantley's POV

I crossed my arms staring down the pouting brunette in front of me as I sighed. I could feel the headache forming behind my eyes and if this had been five years ago I would have already turned up a beer to combat it. But I would have to settle for a bottle of water and some aspirin once I got finished having the same argument for the second time in a matter of months.

"I can't go Brant," Amber said shrugging her shoulders apologetically. "I have a tutoring session lined up for some of the summer school kids and I can't miss that."

"I call bullshit," I growled lowly glaring at her as she rolled her eyes at me. "I heard about this same song and dance in April over the ACM awards. I have a girlfriend, whom I would like to show off, but I can't get you to go to any of these things with me. Like it or not Amber, it's part of my life now."

"Fine," she snapped putting her hands on her slim hips. "I don't like the spotlight okay! All those people watching and looking. Judging. The last date you had to any of these was Jana and you know I will get compared to her!"

"Are you fucking kidding me!" I snapped throwing my hands up pacing my kitchen. "Baby, my life isn't the small venues and clubs anymore! These appearances are something that is expected of me and if you are gonna be a part of my life, which I would like you to be, you need to accept that."

"I don't know if I can," Amber whispered looking down at her hands. My jaw almost dropped to the floor. She had to be fucking kidding me right now. She was the one who pursued me first. Ask me if there could be another chance. I had gone for it after Riley had pushed just a little and then she pulled away saying it was time to try and make her marriage work. She showed no signs of ever leaving Jackson now since Ashley had let it slip they had been trying to start a family. So, I buried the hurt and tried to move on with my life. I braced my hands on the counter looking at my girlfriend as tears welled up in her eyes. "I really don't know if I can."

"You knew this was my life when we started this again Amber," I murmured shaking my head with a sigh. I heard her sniffle as she wiped at her eyes. "Why put either of us on this road if you couldn't handle it?"

"I thought I could," she said shrugging her shoulders. "But we are both different than we used to be."

"What you mean is I'm different," I snapped trying to control my temper. "I'm not drowning in a bottle or popping pills left and right. I actually got my shit together. Is that what it is? You worry the sobriety isn't going to last. I mean I get it. We'd been down that road before and didn't take me long to fall off the wagon. But dammit Amber, it's been almost four years! It's fucking sticking this time! I fight every damn day to make sure it does!"

"I know," Amber snapped back. "And I am so proud of you. I just can't handle the rest of your life. The constantly being gone. The demands on your time. I like it when you are here!"

"Then pack a damn bag and go with me!" I yelled in frustration yanking my hat off and tossing it on the counter between us. "I only beg all the damn time. If this is going to work, you have to meet me halfway!"

"I can't," she said wiping her eyes and shaking her head. I was about to ask her what she meant when my phone rang in my pocket making my back go rigid. As "Sweet Child of Mine" played I tugged it out of my pocket my eyes widening in disbelief. I hadn't really talked to Riley in months. I stared at the screen for a second before swiping my finger to answer.

"Riles?" I asked unable to keep the shock out of my voice. I could hear noise in the background that sounded like she was driving. What made me pause was the sniffles I could hear. Fuck, something must be wrong. She'd taken to talking to Ashley more over the last year than me. I turned around putting my back to Amber not giving a shit how rude it was at the moment, my best friend needed me. "Riley, honey what's the matter? I can tell you are crying. Where are you?"

"Bbbbbb...." She stuttered taking a deep breath her voice sounding so heart broken in my ear. Swear to God if Jackson had done something to her I would kill him. "I hate to call but I need you. Any way I can get you to meet me at our spot? Shit! You are probably on the road aren't you. Shit, I'm sorry. I shouldn't......"

"Riles," I growled cutting her off. "I'll see you there. Twenty minutes good?"

"Yes," she whispered quietly making me worry even more.

"Alright, be careful and I will see you soon," I said quietly before hanging up the phone and turning around to meet Amber's pointed look head on as I slipped my phone back in my pocket. She shook her head. "What? You know damn good and well Riley is my best friend."

"Also forgetting she is your ex-girlfriend as well," she sighed wiping at her eyes. "Always running to see about Riley's needs. That's another reason right there that this can't work."

"What?" I asked in disbelief. "I have hardly talked to or seen Riley in months! She's fucking married remember!"

"Still doesn't mean you don't still love her deep down," Amber said looking at me intently. I had no words to argue. Yes, I loved Riley, truly and deeply but she wasn't mine to have anymore. I had fucked that right up a long time ago. It was Jackson's ring she was wearing and his last name. "See you can't even argue me on it."

"Amber," I sighed walking around the counter and grabbing my keys shaking my head. "Look, I need to check on her and I will be back, and we'll finish this conversation okay."

I had gotten two steps toward the door when I heard her soft voice speak behind me.

"And I won't be here when you get back Brantley," Amber called out to me sadly. "You just made my decision easier by running to her."

"Well," I snarled coldly as my hand touched the door knob. "If that's the way you feel then I guess I will see you around." I yanked the door to the garage open and slammed it behind me before striding angrily to my truck. Twenty minutes later I was turning down the dirt road heading to a back part of Potts Farm. I drove a little further stopping to park my truck beside Riley's black SUV and slammed the door before jogging through the pasture to the huge oak tree in the middle. I paused as I got to the tree to run my hand over the carved initials in the middle of the tree.

I had a flashback to the fifteen-year-old kid who thought he was on top of the world by taking a pocket knife and carving B.K.G. + R.N.W. into the wood. I heard a low sob and stepped around the tree the picture I found broke my heart. Riley was leaned back against the tree with her eyes closed as tears streamed down her face. I tried to figure out why in the hell she had on a loose black and red flannel over her dressy looking shorts and top. Then again, Riley was cold natured.

I stepped closer to ease down beside her. Riley's eyes flew open when she realized I had sat down next to her. I automatically opened my arms and she scrambled into my lap burying her face into my shirt as the damn broke loose on her sobs. I wrapped my arms around her tight as her back shuddered with each sob. My nerves were shot with worry because this was not like Riley at all. I lifted my hand to run through her blonde hair gently just letting her cry it out for a minute.

"Riley honey," I said softly brushing a kiss over the top of her head. "What's wrong? Please you are scaring me. Are you okay?"

"No..." she hiccupped shaking her head. "No... I am not."

"What happened?" I asked slipping my hand under her chin and tilting her head up to look at me. She had mascara trailing down her face and her grey eyes were bloodshot and puffy from crying. I wiped her cheeks slowly with the back of my hand as she took a deep breath. "You know you can tell me anything."

"IIIII....." she stammered biting her lip and looking down. "I found out I can't have kids today."

"What?" I asked in shock as Riley looked up at with tears welling in her eyes again. "Baby, I am so damn sorry."

"It is what it is, I guess," she sobbed wiping at her eyes. I could see the utter devastation on her face. Riley had always wanted a family. It used to be something we talked about when we were younger. "The worst thing is B.... Jackson, he seemed relieved."

"That asshole," I growled feeling my blood pressure rise. "I thought he wanted to start a family. Least that's what Ashley had told me."

"Guess he was just placating me and miraculously got an out," Riley whispered drawing in a shaky breath. "Said we were both too busy anyhow."

"Want me to shoot him?" I asked raising an eyebrow at her. "I will gladly do it. Say the word."

"No," Riley sighed. "If I wanted that I would do it myself. Bastard swears my golf swing sucks but I know I could shoot the damn golf ball out of his hand with perfect aim."

"Fucking right you could," I said with a chuckle earning me a small smile from her as the tears started to subside. "Why don't you get a second opinion?"

"No," Riley said shaking her head quickly. "Hearing this once is enough B. I can't handle hearing it twice. I'll process it and move on. I'll make it. I always do."

"Riles, baby girl," I said softly and she closed her eyes. "You shouldn't settle for anything but the best. That's what you deserve sweetheart."

"I'll be fine B," she murmured trying her best to put on a false front for me. But I knew better. She was completely and utterly devastated. "You always said I was a one of a kind woman. Guess I am just one who's shit doesn't work right. The one thing as a woman I am supposed to be able to do, and I can't. But enough about me. I am so damn sorry for pulling you away. I probably shouldn't have called. I know you're home time is sparse these days and you were probably busy with Amber. Shit...she's soooo pissed at me......"

"She's gone," I answered cutting off Riley's babbling. I cut her off with a look when she started to speak again. "Before you even try and think this is your fault, we were already arguing before you even called. Told me she wouldn't be there when I got back. If I am honest, I saw it coming. I just stubbornly refused to see it. She doesn't like the way my life is now, and I can't and won't change it."

"I'm sorry Brantley," Riley said with a sigh then smirked as she lifted her hand to push my chest. "You..stubborn...never."

I noticed the wince when she pushed me and gripped her right arm before she could yank it back. She yelped when I put a little pressure on her wrist. My eyes narrowed as Riley's widened in fear. Stopping her with a look I gently threaded my fingers through hers and pushed the sleeve of her shirt up with the other one. I saw red at the darkening bruises on her wrist. I could distinctly see the fingerprints on her tan skin. I looked up at Riley as she started trembling from the thunderous look on my face. I knew it wasn't because she was afraid of me. Riley had put me on my drunken ass a time or two in our younger years when I needed it. Back before she lost the confident girl she used to be. She was shaking because she knew what was coming out of my mouth next.

"He's a dead man," I said slowly and coldly. Riley started shaking her head quickly as she clutched my arm as I pushed to my feet dropping her hand. She jumped up diving after me as I turned to stalk to my truck. I had one mission on my mind right now as the red haze surrounded my vision. That was driving that Raptor straight to Atlanta and putting a bullet in Jackson Deveraux's skull. The smug bastard had pissed me off for years and I finally had a reason to light into the mother fucker. Riley wrapped both slim arms around my waist digging her heels in making me stumble. I lost my footing and face planted into the grass as Riley landed in the middle of my back with a squeak. "Dammit Riles! Let me up!"

"No," she hissed in my ear pushing off me to dart to the truck. I knew she was going after my truck keys. Fuck that. She grabbed them, I had no qualms about jacking that flashy Range Rover of hers. I grinned evilly knowing there was for sure a pistol under the driver's seat. I bought the damn thing for her myself. I jumped up chasing after her quickly catching her since my legs were longer and wrapped an arm around her waist tugging her back against me. Riley wiggled trying to throw an arm back into my ribs.

"I'm going Riley Nicole," I growled lowly in her ear. "He's fucked up and you know it. Pisses me off to see a man put his hands on a woman and you fucking know it. Another thing entirely for him to put his hands on you!" Riley ducked out of my arms spinning around to brace both hands on my chest pushing me back. I couldn't help but smirk down at her as she couldn't budge me. Earned me a hard kick in the shin. The tears streaming down her cheeks is what stopped me.

"Brantley please, please, please," she begged looking up at me. "I am begging, don't lose your temper!"

"Too late!" I roared trying to push past her.

"He's not worth it B!" Riley yelled stomping her foot as I stalked past her. I stopped and whirled around throwing my hands up glaring at her as we stared off. Riley was crying so hard she could barely breathe but didn't wipe the pissed off look off her face.

"No! But you sure as hell fucking are!" I roared my hands shaking as I balled them into fists. The last damn person I ever expected to find bruises on and there they were.

"No I am not B!" she yelled at me running towards my truck. "I'm not worth going to jail over!"

I stalked over just as Riley had climbed in the driver's seat of my truck and grabbed her hand to keep her from grabbing the keys. She growled at me as I lowered my head tugging her against me.

"It's been a long damn time since I put a hand across your ass Riles for that mouth," I growled darkly in her ear making her freeze. "Don't you ever....and I mean ever tell me you aren't worth something again. Or across my fucking knee you will go. Fuck, you are my whole damn world woman. So yes, you are worth it. I'd do it in a heartbeat and never hesitate. As long as it meant you were safe."

"Please don't," she pleaded looking up at me wrapping her fingers into my t-shirt tugging. "I can't lose you like that. So please, just let it go. I am begging you."

"Fine," I grumbled through clenched teeth sliding a finger under her chin tipping her face up to look at me. Her bloodshot eyes were killing me. All the fight went out of her as she slumped against me. "But mark my words Riles, he ever does it again. I will kill him. I wish you would leave him."

"It's not that simple and you know it," she mumbled resting her forehead on my chest with a sigh. "I'm so damn tired. God am I tired B."

"I can imagine sweetheart," I said wrapping an arm around her. My phone chimed in my pocket and I tugged it out glancing at the messages and couldn't help but roll my eyes. I dropped a kiss onto the top of Riley's head. I reached around her and pushed the console up then nudged her over. I held my hand out palm up. "Give me your keys and I will leave them on the driver's seat and text Kolby to come get it. Let's head to the house."

"Umm..." Riley said biting her lip looking at me as she handed her keys over. "I doubt that's a good idea. You know girlfriend and all." I rolled my eyes and snorted as I turned around opening her passenger door and laying the keys on the seat. I walked back over climbing in the truck shutting the door as Riley watched me. I drummed my fingers on the steering wheel for a second before answering.

"Not any better considering you have a husband," I said with a sigh making Riley roll her eyes. I got her point. We had done a whole lot worse knowing she had a husband. "But to answer you question. I am now currently free as a bird. One of those texts was from Amber confirming she was done. Had left her key from when she'd stay over on the counter and grabbed the few things she had there. The second one was from Kolby who had pulled up as she was storming out wondering what I did now. So like I said, lets head to the house. You need some rest and peace and quiet. And I need my best friend."

"You okay?" Riley asked laying a hand on my arm as I cranked the truck and backed around to hit the road. I shrugged my shoulders as I took off slinging gravel just to make her smile.

"Does it hurt a little," I said looking over at her. "Yea it does. But I will be honest. I saw it coming just refused to see it. Had my reasons for hanging on you know."

"Yea," Riley whispered then shifted to lay her head on my shoulder. "I do."

Go On....Run That Mouth....

Brantley's POV

I jerked awake hearing a pounding on the front door. I glanced over at Riley still sleeping peacefully on her side curled up in a ball then gently eased away from her slipping out of the bed. I stretched with a yawn as I padded down the stairs to find out where the damn fire was. I swung the front door open to be met with a clearly grouchy and hungover Ashley. One of Eli's t-shirt swallowed her petite frame that was paired with a pair of leggings. Her blonde her was pulled back in a ponytail and her dark sunglasses covered her eyes. I almost made a smart ass remark about look what the cat drug in but the damn woman read my mind and held a finger up stopping me. I sighed leaning against the door frame looking down at her. I knew why she was here.

"I need more time Ash," I muttered as she pulled her shades down to glare at me. Swear it was like a game of hide Riley when she was in town at times because trying to keep her mama in the dark. Then other times Riley just said fuck it, never let her mama know she was in town and hid her SUV in the garage never setting foot off my property. Ashley growled and stalked past me, tossing the bag in her hand near the door and turning to look at me.

"I'll buy you what I can BG," she muttered shaking her head. "But just so you know, Eli is pretty sure Jackson has someone following her. He noticed it last night. Got Kolby to drive off in Riley's Rover since the windows are so dark. Car that was parked across the road pulled right out behind him."

"Fuck!" I snapped running a hand over my face. "That man knows he's just being a selfish jackass now. We both know she has begged him for a divorce and only wants to walk away with her business. Shit, she's more than entitled to half of what he has but she won't take it. But that son of a bitch won't sign the papers. Ashley, I have tried, begged, and pleaded with her to leave him. But she won't because of me. Afraid of what he will do and try and ruin my career."

"She's right you know," Ashley said giving me a pointed look. "He would do it in a heartbeat just for spite. Has never liked you. Always seen you as a threat."

"Ash," I muttered. "I wouldn't have a damn career without her. Hell she's been my damn song writing inspiration for years. I've got to find an out for her. Last night was the last damn time she comes to me doubting herself."

"She broke didn't she?" Ashley asked as I closed the front door and leaned back against it. I nodded slowly. "Any new bruises?" She let out a sigh of relief when I shook my head no. I knew I got a damn good look last night to know for sure. I really wanted to head back up those stairs and curl back up with Riley more than anything. She studied me thoughtfully for a second. "What I want to tell you to do is hold a damn pistol to his head making him sign those fucking papers. Did you know he even hates her seeing me and the kids? Her own god kids now! Says it gives her ideas and will just hurt her since the doctor told her it's next to impossible. That was one of the reasons she sucked it up trying to make things work with him when you and Amber got back together. Then she got hit with that low blow. Hell he doesn't like the fact she sees me and Eli because we are close to you. He doesn't want her, but he likes having that control. Hell B, he knows she still sees you and she knows all about his affairs. But because you are in the spotlight, he uses that advantage to hang over her head and keep her close."

"Ash, I don't know what to do," I said shaking my head sadly. "On one hand I want to respect her wishes and do like she's asks. Hell, she's talked me down from killing him a few times. I can't hold back much longer. Not when everything in me is screaming she's yours. Go beat his ass and just take her. To hell with the blowback. You know, I'd do it in a heartbeat if I wasn't so afraid I would lose her for good over it. I know what we are doing isn't right. So does she, but for now, I will take what I can get. It's my own fault she's in this fucking sham of a marriage in the first place. Me and my addictions screwed up not only my life but Riley's too."

"You didn't screw it up B," Ashley admonished me with an eye roll tapping her foot. "Jackson just happened to come along when she was so damn vulnerable with facing losing her dad. She was stretched then with that, working, helping Lainey, and worrying about you. Yea, it isn't right. But if Eli and I, PJ, Kolby, and your own mama, didn't know exactly how things really are, we wouldn't be helping like we do. She loves you. Even after all the fights, the back and forth, and the booze she still does. Her heart is the one thing Jackson never got. May have bonded her to him with a ring and a piece of paper, but that's it. Yea, she did have stars in her eyes at one point thinking she did love him. Didn't take long after Mike passed away for her eyes to start opening. She thought it was too late then."

"You're right Ash," we heard from the stairs making us both look that way seeing Riley standing midway down the stairs her arms wrapped around her. Her blonde hair sleep tousled, her shirt hanging to the bottom of her tan thighs. Riley narrowed her eyes at both of us. "But like I have told you both time and again. It's my fight. Y'all can't fight this for me."

"Riles..." I said but she stopped me with a raised hand.

"No B," she snapped making me narrow my eyes at her tone. "I have to do this on my own. I have to know that I can get out of this myself. You all love and support me. That's what I need you to do. If it changes, I will let you know. I promise." Ashley bared her teeth in a snarl at Riley and I tamped down a chuckle.

"Good," she grumbled pointing a finger up at her. "Handle it! I can't help you keep this charade up forever. Hell, your mama has already called once wanting to know why you aren't answering your phone. Told her you were busy with Tinsley. And mark my words Riley Nicole, the next time that rat bastard lays a finger on you, I'm letting the pit bull over here off his chain. Won't be no begging him not to step in. You hear me?"

"I hear you Ashley," Riley said rolling her eyes. Well someone woke up full of sass this morning. "I know full well there won't be any stopping him this time. He almost tore the bus apart the last time. I'm gathering leverage to hold over his head okay."

"Just be safe please," Ashley pleaded. I saw the smart ass smile spread across Riley's full lips and I knew something was coming.

"Oh..." Riley drawled that smile widening. "We always are."

"Woman...." I grumbled shaking my head pointing at her. "That was your idea to begin with. Even though you know what the doctor said about you. Damn hard headed, stubborn ass, you won't go for a second opinion!"

"One word B," Riley snarled pointing at me. I rolled my eyes. Fuck here we go again. Let's have this argument...again. "Tucson!"

"Dammit to hell woman!" I growled making Ashley laugh as Riley smirked at me. "That was two years ago and a one time thing! Fuck, I wrapped and still got every damn test under the sun run to shut you up! And that only happened because I was pissed you slipped up and banged your husband!"

"I was drunk B!" Riley yelled back her face flushing with her temper. Dammit she was asking for it this morning. "Don't hold that shit over my head!"

"Well then don't bring up Tucson sweetheart," I grumbled as Ashley snickered. "You know what, I am about to put that sassy ass mouth of yours in its place!"

"Pfftt..." Riley scoffed rolling her eyes. "You wouldn't dare."

"Annnddd that's my cue to leave!" Ashley quipped waving her hand up as I stalked past her with determined steps. She yanked the front door open. "Riles, your bag is over here. I'll have a pillow waiting for you to sit on!"

"I won't need it," Riley yelled back as the door slammed shut.

"Fucking right you will," I said darkly as I stalked closer a slow step at a time. Riley's eyes widened at my tone and I saw her swallow deeply. She went to turn and dart back up the stairs but wasn't fast enough when I grabbed her arm spinning her back around. She let out a yelp when I tossed her over my shoulder. "Nope. You asked for it sweetheart."

"Did not!" Riley argued as I stalked up the stairs to my room. "This isn't funny B! Put me down you fucking caveman!"

"You poked the bear remember sassy ass," I said gritting my teeth sitting her on her feet at the edge of the bed. Riley glared up at me in defiance. I leaned closer fixing her with an intense look. "I'll let you pick which knee."

"Dammit B," she muttered trying to back up but stumbled when her knees hit the bed. "Stop playing."

"You know I'm not playing," I grumbled reaching out to wrap an arm around her waist pulling her flush against me. "You can either lose the underwear or I can rip them. Your choice."

"I'm tired, grouchy, and have a damn hangover!" Riley snarled as I felt her body shake. I knew it wasn't from anger either. "I just want a shower and some aspirin. I don't have time for you to go all Boss on me!"

"Then you shouldn't have been running that damn sassy ass mouth of yours. Bring up fucking Tucson," I murmured with a chuckle sliding my hand down her side to slip under her t-shirt slowly pulling it over her head. "You know exactly what that tone does to me."

"You deserve the sassy tone," she challenged until I lowered my head nipping the side of her neck making her moan. She knew I knew exactly which buttons to push. "Told me no last night."

"You know why I did," I murmured easing my hands down her sides letting them slowly drift down before palming a cheek in each hand squeezing. I heard a quiet whimper escape her throat. I lifted her up to eye level to look at me. Riley gasped and braced her hands on my shoulders digging her nails in slightly. I leaned in nipping her bottom lip making her whimper against my lips. "I'll make up for it baby you know that."

"B!" Riley gasped when I tossed her in the middle of the bed and I reached over looping a hand around her ankle tugging her to the edge. "Don't you dare!"

"Yes mam," I warned. "Bend your sexy ass over the side of this bed right now. If you want to be able to walk later, I suggest you don't test me Riles."

Knowing she had pushed me far enough, Riley slowly rolled over rocking up on her knees pushing that pert ass back at me. I hooked a finger in the string of the red lace thong unable to resist as I lowered my head sinking my teeth into the top of that toned right cheek making her yelp.

"Shit!" she hissed as I grinned then tugged the string. "B! Don't you dare rip those!" Too late I thought as the dainty material gave away with a pop. She growled at me and I raised my right hand cupping it just so as I swiftly brought it down across her cheek earning me a moan. "Dammit!"

"That's one," I murmured moving my hand over to pop the other string holding her panties together tugging them out of the way as I wrapped my left hand around her hip. I raised my hand smacking her again. Riley tried to scramble away from me as I yanked her back. "Two and dammit baby you better be still." I drifted my hand over the curve of her hip sliding my thumb down to press on her clit swirling it slowly. I hissed between my teeth at the wetness I found. "Fuck Riles. I swear you get off on challenging me."

"Almost as much as you do by taking control," Riley challenged back rocking her hips against my hand and biting her lip as she looked at me over her shoulder. Locking my eyes with hers, I spanked her left ass cheek hard as I flicked her clit again. I looked down to see the growing red hand prints on her ass and smirked. Riley lowered her head burying her face in the sheets as she whimpered. I slid my finger down burying it in her wet heat and both of us moaned. I moved it in and out feeling her tighten around me.

"Don't you dare cum," I warned her as she rocked against my hand. I brought my hand down across Riley's ass once more making her moan pushing back against me. Fuck. I couldn't take it anymore as I looked down at her bright red ass. Oh she deserved more for pushing those buttons but dammit I wanted her too bad. Slipping my fingers out of her, I stepped back leaving Riley panting on the bed and yanked open the drawer of my nightstand tugging a condom out and kicking my shorts to the side.

I quickly slipped it on and gripped Riley's hips in my hands easing into her wet heat gritting my teeth. Didn't matter how many times I had done this over the years, it always felt like sliding into home. I held still feeling her pulse around me slowly smooth my hand over her right cheek again earning me a moan. I grinned and smacked her again, hard and Riley screamed clamping down on me. I rocked forward leaning down to her ear slowly sliding in and out of her. "I told you, you better not cum baby girl."

"Then stopping fucking teasing me," Riley moaned pushing back against me. "Fuck me B!"

"Fuck you hmmm...." I murmured taking my left hand and wrapping her long hair around my fist tugging her head back gently. I pulled my hips back driving into her hard. Riley arched her back meeting my thrusts sinking her fingers into the sheets trying to find something to hold on to. Picking up my pace I pounded into her relentlessly feeling her skin grow slick with sweat as I would get her almost to that point then slow down before hammering into her again. Woman may claim she was backing away from me for a while, well then, I was damn sure going to make sure she felt me for a few days. Whimpers, moans, a soft scream, and the occasional gibberish slipped past Riley's lips as I swiveled my hips just so keeping her on the edge. Sliding my hands to her stomach I tugged her up making her back arch as her head dropped back against my chest. I sucked the side of her neck before whispering in her ear. "Cum Riles...cum for me right now baby."

Pressing my thumb down on her clit, Riley dug her nails on my forearm as she screamed going over the edge. Her tight, wet, heat clamped down on me dragging me over with a yell. I rested my sweaty forehead on her shoulder as she shuddered against me with gasps my chest heaving against her back. I knew my arms were the only thing holding her up as a delirious giggle bubbled past her lips.

"Well," Riley mumbled her body shaking as nuzzled the side of her neck with my beard a smirk spreading across my lips. "Was I saying I had a problem with you going Boss on me? I'm sorry. I have all the time in the world."

"No you don't," I said with a chuckle slipping out of her feeling her wince. "Besides, you couldn't handle it."

"Oh, I could damn sure try," Riley mumbled as I walked into the bathroom to take care of the condom on wobbly legs of my own. I reached over turning on the shower before walking back in to find her face first on the bed.

"Come on baby girl," I said leaning over to gently pick her up. "Need to get you in the shower. I'd rather spend all day in bed with you, but like always our time is limited. I don't think you have use of your legs yet."

"Nope," Riley said giving me a contented grin asshe leaned her head up to kiss me softly making my heart ache with the tendernessbehind it. I knew I would be glad when she gathered what leverage she needed tobe able to be free. She was mine. Always had been.

Bullet in a Bonfire

R iley's POV

I adjusted my sunglasses on my face as my hair fell forward trying not to wince. I grabbed the handle of my rolling suitcase shrugging my shoulder to settle my camera bag a little better. I had gotten lucky that I was on friendly terms with one of the older managing partners in Jackson's law firm. I was able to get a flight out on the jet they used to travel back and forth to the New York office from Atlanta. I'd lied and told him that an emergency photo shoot had come up in LA that I had to get to. Worked like a charm. Slipping out the front doors of the airport, I glanced around until I found who I was looking for. I gave the imposing man, leaned against the rental SUV with his arms crossed, a soft smile as I walked closer.

"Take the glasses off," PJ commanded in a gruff voice looking down at me. I swear it was like he knew exactly what was wrong. Like he had been expecting it one day. I slowly pulled them down revealing my swollen cheek and bruised eye. I had to give PJ credit, he'd remained calm when I had called him earlier this evening with what time I would land, begging him to come get me and not tell Brantley. "Fuck! RileyBug, there won't be no stopping Boss from killing him this time. The next words out of your mouth better be that you have fucking left him for good. Or I may just be the one to spank your hard headed ass."

"I have. I promise I'm not going back. Though I know there would be no way Brantley would let me anyhow," I murmured with tired sigh. It had been a hell of a day. I'd give anything just to go back to the beginning of the week before I'd left Jefferson heading back to Atlanta. "I need you to take pictures of my face when we get to the bus."

"About fucking time," PJ muttered under his breath taking my bags from me and putting them in the back before helping me in the passenger seat. A short time later we were walking to the bus in the back lot of the amphitheater. I could faintly hear Brantley rocking out in the distance as PJ keyed the code in and motioned for me to climb on the bus. He walked to the back putting my bags down as I sank down on the couch pulling my knees up and laying my forehead on them. I'd put on a pair of leggings with one of Brantley's hoodies that I had hidden knowing I would get cold on the plane. I felt the couch dip and a gentle hand laid on my shoulder. I lifted my head then slipped my phone out of my hoodie pocket handing it over. PJ snapped a couple photos from different angles before handing it back. "Lay down and get some rest. I've got a couple calls to make but I will be right outside."

I stretched out on the couch getting settled and closed my eyes. I wanted to break down, but I blamed myself because I should have found a way sooner to force Jackson's hand and left him. I didn't even realize I had drifted off to sleep. My eyes fluttered open when I heard the bus door open later and looked to see PJ sitting in the chair across from me keeping watch. He pushed to his feet as I heard footsteps then Brantley's voice.

"Alright PJ, what was the rush to get me back to the bus? I know we have....." Brantley trailed off as I slowly sat up. His eyes widened seeing me. "Riley? What's wrong baby?"

"Brantley," I said quietly as tears welled in my eyes. PJ pushed past him turning my face for him to see. I saw the rage instantly flare in his eyes before he turned to swing at the wall behind him. He stopped mid swing almost hitting Ben who had appeared suddenly with Jesse right behind him. I gasped worried that one of them was going to get punched.

" Woah, woah, woah BG!" Ben yelped holding his hands up and ducking. I smothered a giggle at the high pitch of his voice. "Friendlies approaching. Cease and desist throwing punches." He looked over seeing me grinning and then his normal friendly smiled faded when he heard Brantley's deep growl followed by the crack of his knuckles as he got a good look at my face.

"Ohhhh... he's a dead man. Good thing you look good in black RileyBug because you're about to become a widow."

"Shut up Ben!" Brantley roared making me jump as he stalked over pulling me to my feet. " Everyone get the fuck off this bus! Now!!!" He laced his fingers with mine tugging me to his room in the back guiding me to sit on the edge of the bed. He lifted his hand to stroke my bruised cheek softly letting out a deep growl. "Start talking baby and don't you dare leave anything out."

"PJ already has pictures of my face before you ask," I said looking down at my hands. Brantley noticed my rings missing and smooth a long finger over my hand. I let out a shaky sigh before I started talking. "We went to a client brunch earlier today at the country club. The men played golf and you know I was just expected to sit in the cart and look pretty. Good B, that is so not fucking me, and you know it. At least the few times I have tagged along with you and Kolby I spend the whole time cracking up at you two arguing. But anyways, the senior partner and his young wife that Jackson is seeing were there. She kept shooting me these smug looks. I am assuming they were smug. Bitch has had way too much Botox. It took all I had Brantley to not reach across the table and deck her ass just for principle. I mean, I don't give two shits that she is sleeping with Jackson, she can have him. I guess I didn't school my features well enough so when we got home, Jax challenged me on my behavior. We were supposed to be getting ready for a dinner. I lost my shit Brantley. I was just so fed up and tired of what was expected of me. I'm not even me anymore! Then to shut me up and try and make himself look better, he pulled out a set of photos tossing them on my bed."

"What photos Riles?" Brantley asked through clenched teeth his shoulders going rigid as he wrapped an arm around me.

"Eli was right," I answered shaking my head as a tear slipped down my cheek. "He'd had me followed. Has for a while from what he said. Knew I'd really been with you in North Carolina a couple months ago. Latest photos were of me kissing you after I climbed off the bike the other day when you took me back to Ashley and Eli's. I told Jackson fine, then sign the fucking papers and let me go finally. I could walk out that door and he could have his latest bimbo. Next thing I knew, his hand was flying at my face hard enough to knock me to the floor. He stepped over me telling me to get up and get dressed for dinner. I jumped up as soon as the door clicked closed and packed as quickly as I could. Left my rings sitting in the middle of the photos. Called PJ to get me from the airport. I knew that if he finally did that and fully hit me, he would do it again and not stop next time."

"That's it Riley Nicole!" Brantley yelled jumping throwing his hands in the air. He whirled around pointing at me shaking a finger. "I have let you do this your way. I've been supportive even though I have been sick to my stomach afraid this was gonna happen one day. Now we are doing this my way. Where are those fucking papers?"

"In my bag," I answered looking up at him wiping my eyes. I saw the cold calculation in his green eyes and already knew the answer.

"I want them," he snarled looking at me. "Because that son of a bitch is gonna sign the mother fucking things. Because nobody and I mean no fucking body going to lay hands on what is mine and get away with it! I've let you talk me down enough. Not happening this damn time. I will get the papers signed. Don't worry your pretty little head about it at all baby girl. Stay here and I will meet up with you tomorrow at the next stop. I've got some business to take care of."

"Dammit B!" I yelled jumping up as he turned to the closet in the corner. I took a step back as he turned his head at the fury in his eyes.

"No, don't you even think about trying to stop me Riles," Brantley snapped shaking his head as I glared at him. My heart was pounding because I was afraid of what would happen to him. He reached in the closet pulling out a box and typed in the code before pulling out one of his Kimbers out slipping it into the back of his jeans and tugging his black t-shirt over it. "I told you what would happen if he ever laid another fucking hand on you. I've let you talk me out of beating his ass multiple times over the years. Now, get me the papers please."

I sighed in defeat and stepped over to my camera bag on the chair in the corner pulling the packet of papers out of the side pocket. I handed them over meeting Brantley's gaze. He gave me a curt nod.

"Now, I need your keys that I know should be in the same bag," he said with a direct tone. I dug those out handing them over. "Thank you darlin. Alright, I need the code for the alarm system please. When I'm gone don't step foot off this bus unless Jesse or Ben is with you until I get back. Don't push me on this Riles."

"No I will not!" I yelled walking over to push my hands into Brantley's chest. I hit his shoulder one good time making him growl at me. "I will not be the damn reason you go to jail! Don't throw your fucking life away from me!"

"You will give me that goddamn code Riley!" Brantley roared towering over me. "I promise. I'm not going to jail baby. I was going to Atlanta tonight anyhow. Have a radio interview that had to be rescheduled and then flying back to the next stop. So I have the perfect alibi for being in town. I told you that I wasn't going to jail, and I will not go back on my word. So code. Now."

"Fine...." I gritted out staring him down. "1201985."

Brantley let out a snort and rolled his eyes at me.

"Of course," he snickered as I shook my head at him the angry tears slipping down my face. "I'll be back Riles. I'm not losing you again so go ahead and get that out of your head."

"I love you Brantley Keith," I whispered stepping forward to bury my face in his chest.

He wrapped both arms around me holding me tight. I felt a kiss brushed across the top of my head. He slipped his hand up to grasp my chin making me look at him then lowered his lips to mine. "I promise I will come back with those divorce papers signed. Then, you and I can start our life together. No more damn hiding."

"Glad your convinced its will be that easy," I sniffled and shook my head at the dark chuckle that slipped past his lips before he winked at me.

"I can be very persuasive when I want to be baby girl. You know that," Brantley said before kissing me again. A knock at the door made us pull apart. The door opened a second later as PJ stuck his head in.

"We need to head out Boss before we miss our flight," PJ told him as Brantley hugged me again and nodded.

"Get what we needed?" Brantley asked making me curious. I knew the damn pistol was on him. I glanced up at him with a slight trace of fear. I honestly wouldn't put it past him to kill Jackson.

"Yea Boss," PJ said with an evil grin. "Joe got what we needed. He finished that digging you asked for."

"Good," Brantley nodded and kissed my temple. "I'll be back baby girl. Put some ice on that cheek please. You know where the aspirin is at on here. Get some sleep and I will be back as soon as I can. I love you."

"Love you too B," I whispered knowing I would be a nervous wreck until I laid eyes on him again. He gave me another smile over his shoulder before striding out of the room and off the bus. Lord help me, what was he gonna do.

Time Bomb Tickin

Brantley's POV

Dawn had just broken when PJ pulled the rental we had gotten after landing into the driveway of what was about to be Riley's former home in Alpharetta. If she needed a little time and wanted to go to her mama's I could understand. But I was going to do my damnedest to convince her to finally be where she belonged. I stepped out taking one last drag of my cigarette and stomped it out with my boot. I heard a door shut and glanced across the street to see my brother stepping out of his truck making his way over with Eli right behind him. I actually took a cautious step back when Ashley stormed past both of them hurrying over to me. To say that little woman was pissed was an understatement. I could see the fire flashing in her eyes. I held my arms out and she darted into them giving me a big hug.

"Riley okay?" Ashley mumbled against my shirt as I met the concerned look on Kolby's face over her head. Eli looked madder than I had seen him in a long time. I wasn't surprised out of the reactions. Riley was family and always had been. I'd had to threaten Kolby when I called him on the way to the airport to tell him what was going on. He'd wanted to head out and beat Jackson's ass then. I'd warned him this was mine to handle.

"She's fine sweetheart," I reassured Ashley as she stepped back looking at me. "I texted Ben when we landed to check on her. He stayed on my bus with her. Got her to take something to sleep and was curled up under the covers when he last checked."

"Good," Ashley said leaning her head on Eli's arm a venomous look in her eyes. "I can't believe the bastard hit her."

"I can," Kolby said with a scoff. He handed me a manila envelope heavy with papers. "That was on your porch just like PJ said it would be."

"Good," I mumbled nodding my head. I dug in my pocket pulling Riley's keys out. "Ash, while I am dealing with this son of a bitch, will you go upstairs and pack as much of Riley's things as you can? I don't want her to have to come back here if I can help it. "

"Yea B," she answered as I approached the front door finding the right key and unlocking it. I quickly keyed in the code and we stepped inside. I had been by here a time or two over the years with Ashley when Jackson was out of town, so I knew the basic layout of the house. Ashley quietly tip toed upstairs and I headed into the kitchen. Kolby and Eli both knew to stay out of sight until I needed them, or Jackson tried to run. Riley had told me Jackson would be at the house because he had a standing 7:30 tee time at the local golf course with a major client.

I calmly sat down at the table in the breakfast nook placing the divorce papers, the envelope, and my pistol on the table. PJ stood behind me with his arms crossed over his chest. Not even five minutes later I heard the coffee pot kick on starting to brew. Right on schedule a few minutes later I heard footsteps on the stairs then a sleepy Jackson shuffled into the kitchen. PJ reached behind him flicking the lights on. Jackson jumped and whirled around clutching a hand to his bare chest. I was thankful the fucker had pajama pants on.

"How the hell do you get in here!" he yelled at me and I heard a humorless chuckle from PJ as I smirked.

"Riley gave me her key," I said shrugging my shoulders as Jackson glared at me. I met his glare head on drumming my fingers on the wooden table.

"Figures the little bitch would run to you," he seethed and I gritted my teeth. "Seems to be she's been spreading her legs for both of us. Stringing you along but remember, she's married to me."

"Not for much longer," I snapped pushing the papers across the table and pointing at them. "You will be signing those before I leave from here. As for her sleeping with you, mother fucker I know its been two and a half years since you have touched her. Let's not play games Jackson. She may have been married to you, but Riley never stopped being mine."

"Newsflash Gilbert," Jackson said giving me a bored sigh as he turned to fix his cup of coffee. "She married me not you. You were just the other man. And I'd really appreciate it if you would stop sleeping with my wife. Wouldn't look good for me if that got out. You're crazy if you think I am going to let you have her."

"Listen here Jackson," I said standing up and kicking the chair back making it scrape across the tile floor. I braced my hands on the table trying to calm down. "Riley may have your last name, but I've always had the one thing you never got. Her heart. It's my damn name tattooed on her hip. Been there since I asked her to be my old lady when we were eighteen. And let me explain that to you in biker terms, that right there means more than a damn marriage certificate ever could."

"Fuck off," Jackson said slamming his mug down on the counter. "I'm not divorcing her."

"Yes....you...will," I ground out. "Last night was the last time she comes to me with bruises. Finally got the balls to hit her huh?"

"I did no such thing," Jackson stammered glancing around as I growled. He was looking for his exit I knew and let out a low whistle. Kolby and Eli both stepped through the kitchen door each of them leaning against the wall crossing their arms over their chests effectively shutting down that option. He had to get by me and PJ to get to the other door.

"Bruises on her face say otherwise dickhead," PJ snapped from behind. "And don't worry have plenty of photos of it and from the other times too. Like the bruises on her upper arms from last year when she didn't make it back from a shoot in time to make that dinner you needed her at. Accused her of being with Boss here when her plane had actually been delayed."

"All of that is right here," I said tapping a long finger on the envelope on the table. "Along with a few other surprises I have gotten dug up. See, there is this guy named Joe that we've gotten to know working with the veterans. Quit a resourceful guy let me tell you. He has this little spitfire of a wife that can dig up anything on a computer. And I mean anything. Massacred a dude's credit history one time just for pissing her off. Anyways, little Miss Bella rooted out some interesting stuff for me. You better hope I hide all the guns from Riley when she finds this out. She literally will kill you. Found out you paid off your good buddy Dr. Jacobs to fake her medical problems. That cost you a chunk of Granddaddy's money didn't it. I mean scans and everything. The supposed vitamins he had her on, yea was birth control as insurance. Especially until you could make sure the vasectomy you had was working. Turns out, Riley is perfectly healthy. That news right there broke her. She was and still is fucking devastated over it. You never had any intentions of giving her a family."

"And your point being," Jackson grumbled rolling his eyes. "Children would just take up too much of our time. Riley travels a lot as it is. Fine, I will admit it. I never wanted kids from the beginning and that never changed. I just placated her when she came to me begging. I had just ended things with a hot piece of ass that was looking for a good recommendation to law school. I had already suspected something was going on with the two of you. Then she begs me to try and make things work. Let's start a family she whined. So, I let her think that's what I wanted."

"You mother fucker. You have done put my sister through enough hell," Kolby growled lowly from his stance by the door. I clenched my jaw at just how self-righteous Jackson sounded. "Riley did what she did to try and give B a chance at happiness because you wouldn't let her go. Yea, I knew she'd already asked you for a divorce a few months before that and you threw it back in her face she was yours and no one else's. I went with her to the lawyer to pick up the papers. She was prepared to leave you. Then you held the mortgage to her mom's house and your investment in her studio over her head. I mean, who makes their own wife pay them back."

"Sign the papers Deveraux," I snarled. He pushed off the kitchen counter and sauntered over to me.

"No," he growled stepping closer to me with anger in his eyes. He wasn't pissed about her leaving. He was pissed about losing control. I stepped closer almost in his face.

"You will," I said with a malicious grin. Jackson pushed a hand into my chest never moving me. He went to swing at me and I threw my left arm up blocking him before nailing him with a right hook I put every ounce of power I could into the swing. He fell backwards onto the tile floor with a grunt then looked up at me with malice in his eyes as he held his face. "How's that feel hmmm? I owe you about a hundred more for you ever thinking of laying a hand on Riley." Jackson went to try and stand up and I raised my foot kicking up to catch him in the chin sending him sprawling back down. With blood streaming down his face he lifted his head looking at me. "Sign mother fucker."

"No!" Jackson roared jumping up. "I won't give you the satisfaction! I've enjoyed watching you both squirm over the years because I've been the only thing keeping you truly apart! God, I've got my mother in law so wrapped around my finger it isn't even funny. Will break her poor, poor heart when she finds out when Riley completely disregarded her marriage vows. More importantly what is the rest of the world going to think when I release the pictures. Damn, they will make headline news. Your fans will love that! The record label too."

"Go ahead you bastard," I countered with a smug grin as we stared each other down. "I don't give a flying fuck what is said about me! As long as it means that Riley is safe, do what you want to me. But see, I have proof of my own and a very good relationship with my record label president. Every photo of her bruises, the documents from the doctor, the emails and payoffs, plus photos with you and your string of mistresses over the years, Scott has them in hand as well to counter anything you try and throw out at me. Worry of you doing this is what kept Riley here for so long no matter how much I pleaded. So, I was waiting for the opportunity to present itself. That fancy ass law firm of yours won't take to kindly to some of those photos. I mean really, snorting coke off a hooker's bare breasts in Vegas is so 80's Jackson."

Jackson dove at me again and I met him head on throwing every punch I could. I took a solid left to my ribs and let out a grunt when he got lucky enough to catch my jaw with a right. I kept holding back and tackled him to the ground pinning him with my left hand as I pounded my right fist repeatedly into his face. Pushing up I grabbed him by the throat yanking him to his feet and pointed at the table.

"Sign...them," I warned through gritted teeth pushing him back onto the table as he struggled trying to pry my hand free. Jackson still shook his head. Having enough of this, I reached over grabbing my gun and placing the barrel between his eyes. I heard PJ snicker and knew the snort I heard was coming from Kolby. Jackson eyes widened with fear at the sight of me leaning over him with a gun. I wanted nothing more than to cock it back and put a bullet in him. I could feel him start to shake as my chest heaved with anger. Lifting the Kimber, I pulled back whipping it across his cheek hard enough to split the skin. "Now!"

Slowly nodding his head, I eased my hand from his throat and turned him around pressing his head to the table and pointing the gun at the back of his dark hair. PJ calmly walked around us flipping to the appropriate page and sat them and a pen near Jackson's outstretched hand. A satisfied grin spread across my lips seeing him quickly scrawl his name on the dotted line. When he finished and PJ checked it over he nodded at me. I lifted the gun and fisted my hand in Jackson's dark hair raising his head up to slam it back down into the table hard.

"Bout done in here?" Ashley asked clearing her throat from the doorway as I turned to look at her. "I've got her stuff packed. Or what I knew she would just have to have for now."

"Yep..." I drawled giving her a smirk.

"I'll help her load it up," Eli said. "We will drop it off at your house on the way home."

"Sounds good," I said stepping away from the table. PJ stepping close to me with the papers and folder in his big hands. Jackson was leaned over the table his back heaving. Knew the bastard had to be hurting. I shook my head to clear the ache in my jaw as I turned to head to the door.

"Boss!" PJ warned a little too late as I felt a sharp pain in my left shoulder. I whirled around to see Jackson holding a damn knife I had no clue how he had gotten to fast enough as was holding it up to lunge at me again. I lifted my pistol and fired right into his right foot sending him crashing to the ground with a scream. The only reason I aimed there was because I promised Riley I wouldn't be going to jail. Should have put the bullet between his eyes.

"Mother fucker that burns," I groaned reaching up to grab my shoulder the gun hanging loosely in my hand. I walked over kicking the knife out of Jackson's hand as he laid there moaning in agony. "Might want to get that foot looked at you bastard. It's almost a clean shot. Looks like all you may lose is your pinkie toe. Hope you have an excellent story for that." I kicked him one more time in the ribs just to be evil and turned headed to the door. I slipped the gun back under my shirt and gripped my shoulder with a wince.

"Already text Doc to head this way and look at it," PJ said with a sigh. "He's meeting us close to the radio station. How you gonna explain this one?"

"Rolled my bike. That bastard is too afraid of me now to even breathe a word of this," I said with a snicker as Ashley laughed and opened the door to the rental for me. "PJ! Get me out of here before the whole damn neighborhood wakes up."

"Will do Boss," he said with a chuckle and climbing in the driver's seat. "RileyBug is gonna beat your ass for getting hurt, you know that right."

"Maybe once she gets done yelling," I said with a tired sigh holding onto my shoulder to keep pressure there. "I can convince her to nurse me back to health."

"I draw the damn line at going to find her a sexy nurse outfit," PJ grumbled as we sped away. "No way in hell."

"Shit man," I said with a snicker laying my head back against the seat closing my eyes. "Clothing would be optional."

Freedom

Brantley's POV

I climbed out of the SUV with a grunt after PJ parked by my bus. I was glad that when this sucker rolled out tonight it would be headed back to Georgia. I had a two week break coming up and Scott had already warned me to use it to rest. He'd glared then laughed when I had Face-Timed him earlier to show him the damage. We'd agreed to spin the story I had rolled my bike last night after the show. Riley was going to raise hell because the knife had been a clean cut, but Doc had advised me to put it in a sling since he knew my stubborn ass wouldn't stay still and pull out the stitches.

Between the shoulder and my throbbing hands there was no way I'd be able to play the guitar tonight. I keyed in the code with my good hand knowing I had just enough time to grab a shower and something to eat before I needed to get ready for VIP. I needed to have a conversation with Riley first. Jeff just may have to take a chill pill and the show start a few minutes late. PJ handed me the stack of papers before I stepped inside and shut the door behind me. I laid them on the table. I walked further onto the cool bus figuring Riley was in the back since I didn't see her. I nudged the bedroom door open and found her curled on her side reading. She glanced up seeing me in the doorway and tossed the book aside. She sat up on her knees as I walked closer to the bed gasping in shock as a hand covered her mouth once she got a good look at me.

"I'm fine Riles," I said quickly to reassure her. "Doc made me wear it so I wouldn't pull the stitches out of my shoulder."

"What the fuck happened B?" she murmured running her hands over me checking to make sure I was whole herself.

"You gotten any phone calls?" I asked looking down at her.

"Huh?" Riley said shaking her head puzzled making her blonde ponytail swing back and forth. She had been curled up in a pair of loose shorts and one of my Harley t-shirts. She reached up to cup my cheek running her thumb over the bruise. "No one has a called other than Jesse to see if I wanted something from catering. Then a text from you when y'all left coming back. Why?"

"I figured the hospital may have called," I said as a sardonic smile spread across my lips. "Good that fucker had the sense to keep quiet about what happened to him."

"He still breathing?" Riley asked raising an eyebrow at me before lifting my right hand to inspect my knuckles.

"Ummm sorta," I said with a snicker. She put pressure on my fingers making me his and glare at her. I knew from the look she was giving me she wanted an explanation. "Fine... I roughed him up a little okay. He swung at me first the stupid idiot."

"And....." Riley drawled. Fuck she knew me too well.

"Bastard came at me with a knife when I was leaving," I said pointing at my shoulder as Riley's eyes widened. "He may or may not have gotten a bullet to his foot. Only reason it wasn't between his eyes is I promised I wasn't going to jail."

"Dammit B!" Riley grumbled throwing her hands up glaring at me. Yep, I thought smugly. She didn't give a damn that Jackson got his ass beat, but she was pissed as hell that I came back with more than a scratch. "You come walking back in with your damn arm in a sling, hands busted up, and favoring your ribs. Don't think I didn't notice that. I told you to be careful! See how well you listen to me!"

"Well baby," I said in a calm voice putting a big smile on my face making her growl at me. "Since you are so worried about me, then you can nurse me back to health now. Maybe get you one of those sexy nurse outfits with the short skirt and fishnet stocking. Mmmmmm.... I'm thinking red crotchless underwear. That would be hot. Could replace the thong I snapped the other day."

Riley narrowed her eyes at me before pushing my left shoulder making me wince and curse under my breath. I was due for some more Tylenol soon. She pursed those pink lips at me making me want to catch the bottom one between my teeth.

"Yep," Riley said rolling her eyes at me. "You are in such top notch condition right now. Let me tell ya."

"It doesn't matter," I said quietly wrapping my good arm around her waist and pulling her close. "I got what I went after sweetheart. His signature is on those damn papers."

"You mean...." Riley gasped as her eyes welled up with tears as she looked up at me blinking. "I'm finally free."

"Yes mam," I whispered giving her a soft smile and kissing her gently as she clung to me tears slipping down her cheeks. I tasted the salt on her lips from her tears as I pulled back. "Other than getting the judge to finalize them you are."

"Oh god B!" Riley sobbed as I sat down on the bed and carefully laid back for her to curl against me. Her back heaved with her cries for a second then she lifted her head looking at me wiping them away. "I never thought I would see this day. How soon can they be finalized? I want to be rid of Jackson once and for all. At this point I would walk away without anything. Even my studio if means I can be done. Do I have to go back there ever?"

"I will make some calls Monday," I answered smoothing a hand up and down her back. "See what I can find out. And no, not unless you want to. Ashley packed up what she figured you would want. She and Eli were taking it to the house. You can get it from there when you are ready. I didn't know if you'd be heading to your Mama's or that loft above your studio space."

"I want to go home," Riley said glaring at me fiercely making my heart skip a beat. "And that right there Boss, has always been and always will be with you."

"Well..." I murmured giving her a soft smile with a chuckle as I leaned up to kiss her. "I was kind of hoping you would say that." I broke the kiss a minute later giving her a look as I bit my lip. "As much as I want to continue this baby, I have to get ready. I was already short on time as it is. There's also something you need to see. It's in an envelope on the table in there. Go through all of it okay. I'm going to get a shower and start getting ready for VIP."

"B," Riley said in a shaky voice as I slowly sat up then tugged her to her feet. "You are scaring me."

"Not meaning to baby," I reassured her pressing a kiss to her forehead. "But this is something I know you are gonna need to process on your own. I'll be right here if you need me. Hell, I will walk off the damn stage tonight if that's what you need. But I know you well enough that you will have to look at and read this yourself." I eased my arm from around her giving her a quick pat on the ass before pushing her forward. "Go on."

"Okay, okay," Riley grumbled kicking my leg slightly with her bare foot for good measure as she stalked by. Damn minx, I thought rolling my eyes and letting out a tired sigh. I slipped the sling off tossing it on the bed before kicking my boots off and heading to the bathroom. I peeked around to see Riley sitting at the table with her back to me pulling papers and photos out of the envelope. Her shoulders were already slumped, and she had just gotten started. I backed up heading into the bathroom turning the shower on and closing the door. I made do the best I could getting out of my shirt with only a minor yelp as the stitches tugged but I didn't want to disturb Riley to get any help. I stepped in and turned to keep the bandage as dry as I could. I thought about what she was looking at.

I knew the photos wouldn't really bother her to a point because she had known at the other women for years. Finding out about the first string of girlfriends is what had sent her running home to her Mama's for a while towards the end of mine and Jana's relationship. I'd already known she was cheating on me with her co-star and had really on let Rich and Scott talk me into taking it as far as I did because I was finally clearheaded and thought I'd lost Riley for good.

Riles had been determined to leave Jackson then, but he sucked her back in. What I was worried about was the information about her health. Riley had been devastated finding out she couldn't have kids, and then it turned out to be a lie. That's what was going to send her over the edge no matter how much relief she had over him signing the papers.

I rinsed off and stepped out drying off then wrapping the towel around my waist with a grimace. I opened the door and walked towards the kitchen as quietly as I could. I paused when I saw Riley sitting there as still as a statue, her slim shoulders rigid and her body visibly shaking with anger. I went to take a couple steps to her and she stopped me with a raised hand turning to look at me. Her eyes were red rimmed and her face tear stained but her gray eyes had murder in them.

"You should have killed him," she snapped harshly running a hand over her face taking a deep breath. "There is a special place in hell for that bastard."

"Baby, you want.." I started to stay when she cut me off by jumping up and walking closer.

"No," Riley said shaking her head cutting me off. "I don't want to talk about it right now B. I can't. Give me a little time okay. Come on, I'll help you get dressed. PJ dropped off some Ibuprofen for you while you were in the shower."

"Riles.." I went to argue with her and she shut me down again threading her fingers with mine tugging me to the back. I grabbed the jeans a cut off Bulldogs shirt that would hide the bandage while Riley pulled out a pair of socks. I felt like a damn two-year-old as she helped me get dressed. She remained silent the whole time only poking my stitches once when I tried to stop her from pulling my shirt on. I much more preferred her tugging my clothes of but I would be damned if I told her that right now.

I was too afraid of what she would do. It was never a good thing when Riley shut down like this. Meant a hell of a meltdown when she did break. When she got the sling looped over my arm I stepped over grabbing my cologne spraying some on then my hat. Just to aggravate Riley I spun it around backwards and gave her a wink. She rolled her eyes and stood on her tiptoes giving me a quick kiss.

"Go on before you are late," she muttered pulling back as I looked down at her with worry. She huffed out a breath at me. "I'll be okay B. Go do your job and kick ass. I'll be out there in a little while okay."

A while later Riley came walking up ,PJ right by her side, backstage where the boys and I were in a huddle about to say the prayer as the crowd got warmed up. She slipped under my good arm laying her head against me as Jesse said the prayer. When he was done I looked down at her and noticed she'd went a little heavier on the makeup than normal to cover up most of the bruises. The ice had helped with the swelling some. I heard the opening video start and leaned down kissing her deeply as she clung to me.

"Love you," I whispered against her lips making her sigh.

"Love you too," she said pulling back giving me a wink. "Now, go kick ass outlaw."

Getting It Out In The Open

Riley's POV

I sat staring out the window as Brantley turned into the driveway at Mama's. He put the truck in park and reached across the console to lay a hand on my arm making me jump. The bus had barely been stopped and I had told him I needed to go see Mama. He'd tried to argue with me that I needed to get some sleep first, but I'd stubbornly crossed my arms glaring at him until he'd walked in, unlocked the house, put our bags down, and came back out with the truck keys. I hadn't slept at all on the way back to Georgia. I had either stared at the ceiling or watched him sleep as the miles ticked by. I knew I had to tell her what had happened before Jackson even got the chance to try. I glanced at the time and knew she would be sitting out back enjoying her coffee before getting ready for church.

"You sure?" he asked as I turned to look at him nodding my head. We climbed out and made our way to the gate leading to the backyard. I could hear Mama chattering away and sighed in relief that Ms. Becky was back there with her. I knew she could help Mama see reason if I couldn't. We stepped inside the yard letting the gate swing shut behind us. Mama looked up from her coffee cup pushing her hair out of her face. Her eyes widened in surprise as we approached the table.

"Riley baby," Mama said in shock as I sat down. I glanced over looking at Ms. Becky seeing her lips flatten as Brantley settled a big hand on my shoulder standing behind me. She knew something was up as she noticed his hands then trailed her eyes up to his left arm that I had argued still needed to stay in the sling one more day. Mama narrowed her eyes at me and I could see the worry there. "What's going on? I was gonna call you in a few minutes. Jackson had just text me to see if you were here. Where have you been?"

"She's been with me Ms. Lainey," Brantley spoke up before I could his hand tightening on my shoulder. "Show her Riles."

"Show me what?" Mama huffed and as I raised my left hand to pull off my sunglasses she beaded in that I wasn't wearing my wedding rings. "Where are your rings young lady?"

"On my bed at Jackson's house. I'm divorcing him Mama," I muttered and slipped my glasses off. She gasped covering her mouth when she got a good look at my bruised face. I had covered it up pretty well before going backstage last night but hadn't bothered to this morning. I watched all the range of emotions travel across her face as she processed what I was saying. Jackson had her so bamboozled she didn't know which way was up when it came to him.

"But y'all were so happy!" Mama exclaimed throwing her hands up. "Were you cheating on him?"

"Yes mam," I whispered lifting my hand up to rest on Brantley's as I looked down at my feet. He threaded our fingers together. "I won't lie. I have been and for quite a while. However; your precious Jackson was the one who slipped first and quiet often I might add. We've had separate rooms for a while and he even had a bachelor pad downtown near the firm. I've been trying to get him to sign divorce papers for the last few years and he wouldn't."

"Well of course not, he loves you," Mama argued and Ms. Becky sat her cup down shaking her head. "If you were with Brantley, then you got the bruises from that bike accident I read about this morning?"

"No Mama," I snapped pointing at my face tears welling up in my eyes. "B didn't roll his bike. Jackson hit me. That's what happened. I packed my shit so fast Friday afternoon after he did and caught a plane to Brantley."

"He's gonna know you run to him," Mama muttered I could see her trying to process all this.

"Are you surprised?" Ms. Becky said fixing Mama with a pointed look. "Lainey, are you that blind honey? Those two right there act more married than she and Jackson ever did. They've always loved each other. So of course Riley would run to the one man who makes her feel safe." She looked up at Brantley with a knowing look. "He still breathing?"

"Sorta," Brantley said with a snort shrugging his shoulder. "We may or may not have had a discussion over this."

"You knew about this?" Mama screeched whipping her head around to glare at her best friend.

"Yes," Ms. Becky said calmly fixing Mama with a stare. "Stop glaring at me. I've know about the two of them for a while. How do you think Brantley always knew she was home if she hadn't already told him? I let him know. I found out a few years ago by stumbling upon them and yes, I read them the riot act. Then Riley explained to me more about Jackson that even you don't know Lainey."

"How could you not tell me Becky!" Mama snapped tears glittering in her eyes. "You're my best friend. Why am I the last to know about my own daughter?"

"Lainey, the one time I tried, you brushed me off and got mad because I hinted at the fact Jackson wasn't the man you thought he was," Ms. Becky said with a grim sigh. "I knew then until Riley came out and showed you the proof you would always think that idiot hung the moon."

Mama sat there minute not saying a word and glaring at me. I felt my heart crack at the disappointment in her eyes. Growing up, I had wanted nothing more than to have a marriage like her and Daddy one day. To have someone to love me like that. I wiped at my eyes with my free hand.

"This the first time?" she questioned as I lifted my head meeting her eyes. I bit my lip shaking my head.

"No mam," Brantley grounded out between clenched teeth. "It's not. I've found bruises on her before. On her wrists and upper arms. Every time I tried to get her to leave him. This is the first time he ever went for her face though."

"Mama," I said choking back a sob as the tears fell harder. "He paid off a doctor to convince me I can't have kids. That's why I would get so upset when you would bring up having grandkids. I thought I couldn't have any."

"Riley," Mama gasped covering her mouth as tears fell down on her own cheeks. I felt the hand on my shoulder slide around to wrap his arm loosely around my neck as I lifted my hands up to grip his arm. "Oh my baby. Bless your heart. I wish you had come to me and told me. I love you baby girl and there is nothing and I mean nothing and no one that I would ever believe over you. I feel like such a fool. I don't know what that jackass said to make you think I wouldn't be here for you but you are my daughter. I'm always here for you. Your daddy and I loved you so much. You will always be my heart."

"It was my mess," I muttered swallowing down another round of tears. Ms. Becky smirked at the low growl I heard behind me as I sighed.

"How did that discussion go baby boy?" Ms. Becky asked giving Brantley a look. "Looks to me like you did a little talking with your fists."

"Just a smidge Angel," he said with a snicker. I rolled my eyes and leaned my head back to rest on his stomach. "I took the decision out of her hands the minute I laid eyes on her face. Jackson however did sign the divorce papers. Finally. Gonna make some calls tomorrow to find out just how soon this all can be over."

"And your shoulder?" Ms. Becky prodded slight worry in her eyes.

"Asshat came at me with a knife when I was trying to leave," he grumbled, and Mama eyes widened.

"You know you can always stay here sweetheart," Mama said giving me a watery smile. "Kind of like the thought of having you around a little more."

"I know Mama," I murmured then turned my head to look up at Brantley as he gave me a soft smile. "But I'm going home. Finally."

"Well then," Mama said standing up wiping at her eyes and walking over to me. I stood up as she cupped my cheeks in her hands. "give me a hug baby and get yourself home and get some rest. You look dead on your feet. But I want to know how this goes from now on do you hear me?"

"Yes mam," I whispered as she tugged me to her enveloping in her warm arms as the tears started again. "I'm so sorry Mama that it happened like this. But I just wanted you and Daddy happy and that was the last good memory I had of making Daddy happy. Jackson used it and twisted it to suit his needs."

"But you weren't happy sweetie," Mama whispered stroking a hand up and down my back. "That is what is most important. Becky was right and I should have seen it. You two have always completed each other. Lord if anyone had asked when you came strolling in at eighteen wearing his leather jacket and his name tattooed on you, I would have told them they were crazy if they thought you two would still be that in love years later. Well, I was wrong and I should have seen it." Mama let me go and stepped up to Brantley laying a soft hand on his cheek smiling up at him. "Thank you for what you have done. For always been there for her. I have always been grateful that she never lost you as a best friend. But you gave her moments of happiness when she needed it most in this world. Now, you take her home and make her happy because, blind or not, we know that you love her and she loves you. Hold onto that love with everything you both have and don't let go."

"Yes mam," Brantley whispered leaning over to give Mama a hug and kiss her cheek softly. She wrapped me in another hug before Ms. Becky wrapped an arm around us both hugging us tight.

"Take her home and put her to bed baby," Ms. Becky said with a sigh. "She's gonna need some rest after the last few days. I knew something major had happened when Ashley told me Riley had finally left."

Brantley wrapped his arm around my shoulders and led me back out to the truck opening the passenger door helping me climb in. I slipped in then laid my head on the cool, tinted glass as he climbed and backed out of the driveway. The radio played quietly as I listened to the drum of the wheels on the road. He hit a bump and it was like the damn holding my tears back broke free. I started crying so hard I could barely breathe. My whole body was shaking.

I leaned forward resting my head on my knees as I clutched at my chest sobbing. I couldn't believe I'd been so stupid. How had I stayed for so long? I hadn't been happy. I'd been lied to, cheated on, and hit. I felt a hand loop around my bicep yanking me across the middle of the truck as I heard the engine rev with speed. Brantley turned me gently so I could bury my face into his chest as I sobbed. He smoothed a big hand over my back up and down.

"I'm right here baby girl," he said gruffly as I kept crying. "Just let it all out."

"God," I sniffled looking up at him through the tears in my eyes. "I don't know why you are. Or what I ever did so right in my life to have you here after all I've put you through. But I can't lose you again."

"Darlin," Brantley said glancing down at me intensely. "I promise you there ain't nothing gonna run me off. I am so blessed to have you and I don't know what I ever did for you to give me another chance after all that happened, but you are stuck with me."

He pulled up to the house parking and killing the engine as I looked at him with a small smile spreading across my lips. I knew I could get through anything life threw at me with him by my side. He opened the door and slid out turning around to tug me to the edge of the seat. I stopped him laying a hand on his shoulder as we stared at each other. Green meeting gray and I felt like my whole world was complete.

"Because I love you," I whispered. "Have for as long as I can remember. I honestly don't think I could ever stop."

"And I love you," Brantley said giving me a quick wink and tugging me out of the truck towards the house. He looped an arm around me as we made our way inside. "I haven't ever stopped and I won't."

He lead me upstairs to his room pausing to yank the covers back as I kicked my flip flops off and climbed in settling onto the cool sheets with a sigh. I was so damn tired. Brantley eased the sling off and leaned down for me to help him slowly tug his t-shirt off then kicked his Nikes to the side before crawling in beside me. I rolled to my side facing him as he draped an arm around my waist tugging me closer and twining our legs together.

"You need to get some rest baby," he murmured brushing a soft kiss on my forehead making me sigh as I traced my hand slowly up and down his face. "Been an emotional roller coaster the last few days."

I laid there quietly for a few minutes then the tears came out of nowhere again.

"God B," I whispered tearfully. "How can you do that to a person? I have for so long felt like I was a failure at life. Have felt that way ever since that fucking idiot broke the news to me. Turns out it was all a lie."

"I don't know baby," he murmured stroking a hand over my cheek wiping at the tears. "There are some things in this world I can't explain. But, now you know. And you know that it didn't matter to me either way. I loved you just as much when you told me as I did before. Some people don't know how to love. They just love to control people."

"You're right about that," I growled angrily. I knew it would take me a little time to get over this hurt. "He did that for way too long. I should have listened and went for a second opinion and your ass will be sleeping on the couch if you even think of telling me I told you so. IIII....just...I just couldn't handle hearing it twice. When he told me, it was next to impossible, I saw the little girl I had always envisioned with blonde hair and the prettiest green eyes disappear right in front of me like a puff of smoke. After that, I just gave up."

"Baby," Brantley murmured giving me a reassuring smile. "You can have that dream, but with your eyes and his there was no way you were getting green. Unless......"

"Even though I was married to him," I said giving him a sad smile. "That was what I always saw when I thought about kids. Never changed. I've seen her since I was eighteen years old and someone's drunk ass climbed on the bar at the MC with a fifth of JD in his hand grinning from ear to ear. Told me there was no ifs, ands, or buts about it, I was gonna be your old lady."

"Well then," he drawled with a quiet chuckle. "I sure hope I can give you all your dreams then. Because lord knows you are mine."

"If that never comes to pass," I said softly and lifting my head to kiss him slowly. "I know I will be okay. I've got you and I am finally done with Jackson. That's all that I need baby."

"Baby girl," he said softly kissing me and biting my bottom lip before tucking my head into his neck and sighing. "Rest now. Please. You are beyond exhausted and I need you rested up. We have the rest of our lives to get to living."

Birthday Surprise: Part I

B rantley's POV

"Please dear lord tell me that was the last piece?" Kolby grumbled as I looked over smirking at him. The canopy I had bought was finally put together. Swear he had rolled his eyes once he realize what we had gone to Lowe's for this morning.

Fucker had made the mistake of crashing on my couch last night, so I'd rolled him off it this morning grinning and waving a cup of coffee under his nose to help me get a few things together today. Riley had been in Atlanta the last two days for a couple of appointments she couldn't cancel. So far, she hadn't heard anything from or about Jackson other than him sending someone after her Range Rover since the lease was in his name. She had been pissed but I had just walked into the kitchen as she stood on the porch fuming.

Her eyes had widened before the biggest grin had spread across her lips as I handed her the keys to the Cougar with a smile. I had a few days before I had to go back out on the road and was hoping that she'd cleared enough stuff to be able to go with me. She had text me this morning excited because she had found out her divorce would be final on June 15th.

Had proclaimed finding that out was the best birthday present ever. I had chuckled and text her back that was up for debate. Just three short weeks she would be completely done with him.

"Oh quit your bitching," I said with a snicker standing back to admire our handywork. Kolby stood beside with his arms crossed over his chest grinning.

"She's gonna love it," he said with a chuckle. "Will be especially glad this thing came with mosquito netting. Should have just bought a damn tent. Taken less work."

"So sue me for trying to be romantic," I grumbled punching him lightly in the shoulder. Kolby started laughing as I sighed knowing I sounded cheesy as hell. "Look, Riley has had a rough enough time. She's finally free of Jackson. We can finally be together again without hiding it. Therefore, I will straight up go the whole nine yards man, tux with tails, top hat, roses, moonlight serenade with a string quartet, whatever it takes to make her smile."

"Bro," Kolby said cracking up laughing holding his sides. "If you did that Riley would think you had lost your mind. Ask you who you lost a bet with. Her money would be on Justin for that. I mean come on ain't the exact words to describe that would be "She ain't into wining, dining......". There's a reason that woman's ringtone is "Sweet Child of Mine". I do call dibs on one those fluffy ass pillows you bought."

"Got a point," I said with a chuckle. I pulled my phone looking at the time. "Alright let's get this finished so I can get everything else taken care of. You know what you have to do later right?"

"Yes B," Kolby said rolling his eyes and walking to where my truck was backed in near our tree. "I've only been reminded a hundred times. Smoke a

cigarette and calm your ass down. Geez you are acting like you are propos-
ing or something. Wait... are you?"

"No," I said rolling my eyes shaking my head as I pulled bags out of the
backseat. "I'm not. At least not yet."

Riley's POV

I pulled up to the house hitting the button on the visor to open the garage.
I had gotten the few things I'd needed taken care of. I had juggled a few
appointments to free me up to go on the road with Brantley. I had one in
Nashville next month, but I figured I could talk him into going with me.
I had already put out feelers for an available building in Athens so I could
be closer to the house. I frowned as I looked around outside noticing I
didn't see Brantley's truck. I had thought when I called him to tell him I
was headed in from Atlanta he was here. I was looking forward to curling
up on the deck and enjoying the birthday steak he had promised me.

Jackson had either forgotten my birthday every May or made a big deal
about it. I just wanted quiet and simple. Climbing out of the Cougar, I
leaned in the backseat pulling my purse and camera case out. I had the few
clothes and things I had at my studio loft in the trunk. Brantley didn't need
to know I had to bat my eyelashes at a state trooper on I-85 after he pulled
me over for going ninety. Had assured the officer I would slow down and
why yes it was the same car from "The Weekend" video after he ran the
license plate.

I walked into the kitchen sitting my stuff on the counter looking around
the quiet house.

"Where the hell is that man?" I muttered reaching back to pull my phone
out of my shorts pocket to call him. As I was about to hit the speed dial, I
noticed a deep red rose that was almost black laying on the counter with a

note attached to it. I slipped my phone back in my pocket walking over to pick it up. I sniffed the rose before unfolding the note.

To the most special woman in my life, while you may be another year older. I am thankful that I get blessed with another year of having you in my life. Happy birthday baby. Now, go look upstairs. Left you something on the bed.

I bit my lip as a wide smile spread across my lips and I couldn't help but taking off running to see what he was up to. I darted up the stairs and skidded my way into our room pausing when I saw the black lace sundress laying on the foot of the bed.

I walked over picking it up by the delicate straps shaking my head. I knew it would show up my tans legs. Something that he loved. I saw another rose laying on the bed with a note attached it. This man I swear, I thought smiling as I opened it.

You know you are the love of my life right? If you didn't well then, I plan on showing you every day for the rest of my life. I vow that even when we fight, argue, and aggravate each other, you will never doubt that I love you. Now, put on the dress, spray some of that perfume that makes me think of vanilla cupcakes on, and head to front porch for your next instructions.

I dropped the note on the bed and darted to the bathroom throwing my hair up to keep it out of the way and took a quick shower. I didn't bother redoing my makeup because I knew when it boiled down to it, he preferred me without it. I fixed my hair up in a messy bun leaving a few wisps around my face calling it good as I grabbed the lotion and body spray he had been talking about. Man had made sure I had a healthy supply of it because he loved it. I walked back in our room pulling a black strapless bra out of the drawer slipping it on before tugging the dress on.

I purposely left off the underwear and grinned to myself. Two could play the noooootthhhiiinnn game. I slipped on a pair of my wedge sandals and my long cross necklace with the black diamond earrings Brantley had gotten me for my birthday last year. Grabbing my phone off the bed, a giddy laugh slipped past my lips as I hurried downstairs flinging the front door open. I checked up my hurry when I saw Kolby standing there smirking at me.

"Oh," I said frowning just a little making him laugh.

"What?" Kolby said with a booming laugh before picking me up wrapping me in a massive hug. "Disappointed I'm not your boy toy? Happy Birthday sis."

"Thanks Ko," I mumbled squeezing him back as he sat me on my feet. I narrowed my eyes as he pulled out a note along with a blindfold wrapped around another rose.

"Well," Kolby said motioning at me to open the note. "Get to reading so we can get this show on the road missy. Know how impatient BG can be."

I snickered and nodded my head as I opened the note.

I have no doubt that you look beautiful. Simple has always looked best on you. Bet that black makes your stormy grey eyes glow. Put that blindfold on.....no arguments baby girl. Have a little faith in that I know what I am doing. I love you and see you soon.

"Ready?" Kolby asked as I finished reading and held out an arm to walk me to his truck.

"Any chance you will tell me what he is up to?" I asked looking up at him giving him a wide smile and batting my eyes.

"Hmmmm...." Kolby drawled as he opened the passenger door for me. "Nope." I growled at the answer as he snatched the blindfold out of my hand and wrapped it around my eyes testing to make sure I couldn't see. I felt a soft kiss placed to my forehead before he helped me climb in. "Just relax and enjoy Riles. Promise, you know he will make it worth the guessing games."

"If you say so," I muttered trying to be mad but I couldn't contain the smile on my face.

Birthday Surprise: Part II

R iley's POV

"Kolby...." I growled through clenched teeth from the passenger seat of his truck. I swear if I was I allowed to pull this blindfold off I would look over to see him lazily driving around. I wasn't stupid. He was stalling for some reason or killing time one. I was about to kill him if he didn't get me to Brantley soon. I turned my head shaking a finger at him. "I swear you are driving slow on purpose. Nana Gilbert drives faster than this headed to Bingo!"

"First of all," Kolby said cracking up. "No one and I mean no one stands between Nana and her weekly Bingo game at the Moose Lodge with her cronies. Sis, she smacked the sheriff with her purse the other day for pulling her and Mazie Jenkins over. He let her go with a warning but called Dad to tell him he needed to talk to her. Know what Dad said, told Sheriff John that he would get Brantley to handle it when he got home."

"Well," I drawled with a laugh. "He was the one how bought her the Caddy. She took me for a spin the last time I was home. I had a good grip on the oh shit handle. But seriously, are we there yet?"

"Almost," Kolby chuckled. "Have a little patience?"

"Since when have I ever had that?" I challenged snarling at him. I drummed my fingers on the console and felt a big hand squeeze mine stopping me.

"I promise," Kolby said with a laugh. "It will be worth it. That....and we are here."

I felt my heart pound in my chest a little feeling the truck stop and Kolby parked before I heard him climb out. My door opened a second later and he helped me step out. I could tell it had gotten darker as Kolby held my arm guiding me forward. I felt soft grass brush against my bare legs and wondered just where I was until Kolby stood behind me.

"Have fun sis," he whispered in my ear before untying the blindfold. I blinked letting my eyes focus in the setting sunlight and I lifted my hand covering my mouth with a gasp. Kolby gave me a slight push forward as I looked over seeing Brantley standing a little ways in front of me. I took in the canopy behind him that was right beside our tree. Rows of LED candles surrounding it and setup on the inside. It had a covering around it with what looked like mosquito netting. I walked closer with my heart racing. I took in the man standing in front of me with a soft smile on his full lips. The heather grey t-shirt fit in all the right places giving me a subtle look at the muscles and tattoos I knew that were underneath. Rings on those long fingers that sent shivers down my spine when that cool metal traced along my skin. All too familiar black hat pulled low over his green eyes that sometimes felt like they could see into my soul. In his hand was a single rose like all the others.

"Hi," I said softly reaching my hand out to take it of his hand as he gave me that wide smirk that the ass knew brought me to my knees. Brantley reached over wrapping an arm around my waist pulling me close to him.

"You look beautiful," he murmured lowering his head to place a soft kiss on my lips. "Happy Birthday baby."

"B?" I said with a soft giggle as he threaded his fingers with mine walking backwards tugging me with him. "What have you done?"

"Wanted to do something special for your birthday sweetheart," Brantley said with a chuckle guiding me into the structure and helping me sit down on the mass of pillows and blanket he had set up. He zipped the covering closed and looked down at me laughing as I traced a hand over the softest pillows I had ever felt. I couldn't take my eyes off him as he sank down beside me. I narrowed my eyes as he reached over for his acoustic guitar that was sitting to the side. I smiled because I recognized it as the one I had bought him for his thirtieth birthday. Matte black with his logo on the base in silver with flames around it. Stretching out, I curled up settling my head on one of the pillows as he got the guitar settled in his lap lightly plucking the strings.

"Been a long time since you've sang to me," I said quietly as he smiled at me.

"That it has," Brantley murmured giving me a sly wink. I wasn't naïve, I knew there were songs written about me. A lot that would never see the light of day. But I never got tired of hearing him sing to me. When Daddy had first been diagnosed, I would curl up against Brantley the nights I was too upset to sleep and let him sing me to sleep. At least I did before it all fell apart. He gave me a soft smile before he started to sing.

It's amazing how you can speak right to my heart

Without saying a word, you can light up the dark

Try as I may I could never explain

What I hear when you don't say a thing

The smile on your face lets me know that you need me

There's a truth in your eyes saying you'll never leave me

A touch of your hand says you'll catch me if ever I fall

Now you say it best When You Say Nothing at All

I reached up whipping a tear away that had slipped down my cheek. An old classic from Keith Whitley that had been the first song we had ever danced to. It had been Mama and Daddy's song and she used to play it all the time. I slowly sat up as he strummed the last chord and wiped at my eyes. Brantley's brow furrowed in concern as he sat the guitar to the side reaching for me. Pulling me into his lap so my legs sat on either side of his he brushed a tear away from my cheek.

"Didn't mean to make you cry sweetheart," he said softly looking into my eyes. I lowered my forehead to his shaking my head.

"Good tears," I whispered making him chuckle. "I promise. Best birthday present so far handsome."

"Who said I was done?" he muttered quirking an eyebrow at me. He leaned back bracing one hand on my leg and reaching back to pull a box out from under a pillow. He had them scattered everywhere. He slowly sat back up and placed the box in my hand biting his lip nodding for me to open it. I cracked open the lid and gasped at what I saw inside. Brantley gently took the box from me and pulled the delicate bracelet out holding it up. The thin wires had crystals on it with an emerald in the middle. I studied the clasp and smiled.

"The wires are strings from my guitar," he murmured as he slipped it onto my wrist holding it up. "The ladies over at Spent Round Designs were kind enough to help me with it. The bullet casing for the clasp is from my Kimber and the emerald since its your birthstone, they shaped it like a guitar pic. It has my logo on one side and our initials on the other."

"It's beautiful baby," I whispered sniffling just a little at how much thought he put in to it. "I love it. And I love you. Have a piece of you wherever I go."

"Baby girl," Brantley said with a quiet laugh laying a hand right over my heart then took my hand to lay over his as he looked in my eyes. "That right there is all yours and has always been. So you always have me with you."

"I feel like the last week has been a dream," I confessed shaking my head wryly as those long arms wrapped around me pulling me tighter to him. "Just ready for it to all be over with."

"Not much longer darlin," he said grinning and kissing me quickly. "So, get everything taken care of in Atlanta?"

"I did," I said smiling. "I can go with you for a few weeks before I have another quick shoot. My lawyer told me this was being handled out of court because of who Jackson is so I don't even have to be present. I also had another appointment while I was there. I finally went for that second opinion."

"And?" Brantley asked studying my face. I bit my lip wrapping my arms around his neck.

"She said I was perfectly healthy," I said as a soft smile spread across my lips and he grinned at me. " I know I should have done this sooner. But I showed her the other files and she almost lost her professional cool. But comparing those to the tests she ran, I am fine. I had kept up with the birth control as a back up just because of the situation I was in."

"Sooo,"he drawled as he smirked at me. "What you trying to tell me baby?"

"That once the shit is finally over," I said blushing a little. "I want that family I have always wanted when the time is right and I want that with you. I always have."

"Telling me I can toss that box of condoms out finally sweetheart?" he said giving me a lewd wink knowing he was making my blush deepen.

"Yes you ass," I grumbled pushing his shoulder and making him fall back tugging me with him as he chuckled. Brantley lifted a hand burying it in my hair pulling my face down to nip my bottom lip making me moan.

"Baby," he whispered against my lips as he raised his knees making me fall over his chest and his free hand settled on my thigh pushing my dress up slightly. I rocked my hips against him enough to tease. "I'm going to do my damnedest to give you the life you have always wanted. Smack me and keep me in line when I need it."

"B," I said chuckling against his lips. "As long as I have you, I have everything. Anything else is just icing on the cake."

"Mmmmm..." Brantley murmured flicking his tongue out along my bottom lip. "Icing, damn I should have thought about that." I felt the rough hand on my thigh slide higher and his eyes widened as a long finger brushed against my core. My breath caught in my throat at the heated look that come across his face. "Really baby....nothing? Hmmm...can it be my birthday too?"

Wives of Nashville

R iley's POV

I put my hand on one hip glaring at the man standing in front of me. A low growl slipped past my lips making his eyes widen but they quickly narrowed letting me know he was standing his ground. I had gotten pitched the photo shoot for Nashville Lifestyles a couple of months ago. When you were dealing with the couples I was, it took a little planning to get them together. I held the scissors in my hand up making them do a loud snipping sound and saw the man swallow deeply as his tan skin paled. I had known him long enough he knew I meant business.

"I mean it," I growled lowly. "You cut that shit or I do mister. The hippie vibe ain't working on my photo shoot ideas."

"Guess I should have grabbed the keys to Tyler's motorcycle and a leather jacket to make you feel more at home," the man grumbled glaring at me.

I went to take a step forward raising the scissors with one hand and going for an ear tug with the other when a band of iron slipped around my waist tugging me back. I threw an elbow back earning me a low warning growl that reminded me I better chill. I debated for half a second on just how red he would turn my ass later if I stomped his foot and got free. Then I thought better of it. I sighed and leaned back into the warm chest behind me as everyone else laughed.

"BG man, please, please take them away from her!" BK whined poking his lip out making BCole smack the back of his head as she walked by to hand Olivia back to Hailey. She rolled her eyes at her husband and sighed. THubb was holding his sides and laughing as I felt Brantley chuckle as well.

"I told him he had longer hair than Hailey last week," Tyler said giving me a wink.

"I dunno man," Brantley snickered lowering his chin to rest on my shoulder a wide smirk on his lips. "Think Willie is the only one who can pull the braids off bud."

"Fuck y'all," BK grumbled and went to sit back in the chair to let the hairdresser do something a little different. Better be a ponytail or I was going to beat him.

"You are in deep shit Riley," BCole called out with a laugh as Brantley kissed me on the cheek and stepped to the side to answer his phone. I walked over to snatch Olivia from her to get some snuggles as Hailey checked her lipstick. She grasped the strands of my blonde hair in her tiny fist making me smile. My divorce had been final a month ago and thank the Lord it had happened smoothly. Brantley had been pissed slightly that I hadn't walked away with more after all that Jackson put me through, but I was just glad to be free. I had the boys of FGL lined up first this morning with the other few couples trickling in today and tomorrow.

"Alright..."BCole drawled giving me a wink as she threw an arm around my shoulders. "I see the wedding band is missing thank god. I just have gotten to know you the last year or so with the Tribe Kelly stuff honey, but you could just tell. Now I see you came equipped with a very hot bad boy attached to your hip today. Spill woman."

"BG and I have been best friends since we were kids," I said shrugging as Hailey rolled her eyes at me. I sighed. "We had dated for years and then had a falling out after we graduated high school and were off and on for a bit still until I couldn't handle the drinking. Then Amber came into the picture. I met Jackson, got married to him, my father died. Rock on a few years and I find out he was cheating on me so I left. I've been trying to divorce him for years he just wouldn't let me."

"Still seeing BG on the side?" Hailey asked curiously as my eyes widened. She gave me a soft smile. "No judgement sweetie. It's very easy to see how much he loves you and lord knows we all know he is stubborn. Strikes me that he would take you anyway he could."

"Yea you are right," I said with a sigh and turned my head as I head footsteps approach. My eyes locked with Brantley's as he smiled at me before walking over to harass the guys. "That man right there is the love of my life."

Later that day in the early afternoon I took a long sip of water and grabbed the spare battery the assistant from the magazine handed me changing it out before pulling my long hair up in a messy bun. I heard a high pitched squeal and turned my head to look over my shoulder as a warm smile spread across my lips. I heard a chuckle beside me and turned to see Thomas giving me a smirk.

"That man right there," he said laying a hand on my shoulder and pointing over to Brantley in the corner holding Ava over his head making her giggle as he made funny faces at her. "Was born to be a dad."

"Maybe one day," I said sighing wistfully as Lauren walked up to my other side rolling her eyes. I stuck my tongue out at her making her laugh. I knew Brantley would be in kid heaven today since he'd had Olivia to play with this morning, Willa and Ada right now and I had Carrie and Mike coming in soon so he'd be palling around with Isiah later. "What?"

"Girl please," she snickered as Thomas laughed. I looked back to see Willa running around with that black hat on her head giggling. I quickly lifted my camera up to snap a picture as Brantley darted after her with a laugh, Ava cradled in his big arms. "After all these years of being apart and on the down low, he will have you locked down as quick as he can. From what you were telling me over dinner the other night, it's been final for a month huh?" I nodded and Lauren grabbed my hand holding it up. "Wow..... a month and no ring on that finger, BG is slacking."

"Oh shut up!" I said pushing her shoulder as she snickered. I had gotten to know both Lauren and Thomas over the years and they were some of the few in this part of Brantley's life that knew what had been going on. I tried to get together with her when I was in Nashville. I had even more fun now when we got together because of the girls. Instead of where I once felt sadness all I felt was anticipation. I knew when we would have that one when the time was right.

"She's right you know," Thomas said with a chuckle as we watched B chase a giggling Willa around making growling noises. "I wish you could have seen what I saw the first time I ever met you. You walked into the back room of that venue where we were sitting around picking guitars and his whole face lit up before he tamped it down trying to hide it. Lauren told me you are moving the studio to Athens?"

"Yea," I said with a grin pointing to the middle of the backdrop so they could get in place for the pictures. These two were so easy to get the photos I was looking for because they had so much fun together. And like Brantley and I, they had known each other forever. I motioned for Thomas to wrap his arms around Lauren as I moved around them. She looked over her shoulder sticking her tongue out at him making him crack up. Oh that one would be used for sure. "I want to be closer to the house and yes, before you even make a comment Thomas, I didn't even hesitate to settle my butt in Maysville. Won't be as much foot traffic for the prints that I sell but it will be okay. I figure I will be booking shoots next year around tour dates as much as I can."

"I bet you will," Lauren said with a giggle. "He's going to want you to go with him as much as you can."

"Telling ya," Thomas said with a grin dipping Lauren over his arm making her long hair almost trail the ground as she smiled up at me. "You will be changing your last name to what it always should have been before the year is out."

A week later I was sitting on the cool grass as the sun set. I'd flown out to Ireland the next day after the shoot in Nashville to get some travel photos from around Belfast. Brantley had headed back out on the road and had a string of interviews to do. I had been able to score a few photos of the Game of Thrones set that I knew the perfect person to send them to who was affiliated with the show. I felt my phone vibrate in my hoodie pocket and slipped it out. The cool weather was a stark contrast to the humid heat I would be dealing with if I was back in Georgia. I sat my camera down then unlocked my screen smiling at the text.

BG: Miss you like crazy beautiful. Counting the days until you come home.

RW: Miss you too handsome. Nights have been cool here and only so much I can snuggle under the covers. I need my favorite pillow.

I sighed after a minute when I didn't get a reply back. I tried to mentally calculate what time it was back home but my brain was frazzled from a long day of walking around the cliffs nearby. I was just ready to be back home. There was a time that I lined up shoot after shoot, so I wouldn't have to be home. But I wanted to be there now. The sun was almost out of sight and I lifted my legs up to rest my chin on my knees. I closed my eyes giving myself another minute to enjoy the surprising peacefulness as the night air settled in. My heart almost pounded out of my chest when I felt a presence near me and before I could turn around a long pair of jean covered legs settled on either side of mine. I was about to jump up when I was surrounded by the familiar smell of leather, cigarettes, and home. I couldn't help but smile as I was tugged back into a warm chest.

"Hi," Brantley murmured into my ear then leaning down to kiss my neck. I leaned back into him as I turned to look back at him pressing my lips to his.

"What are you doing here?" I asked giddily against his lips. "I thought you had back to back radio interviews before you could head home."

"I may have begged Mike to reschedule them," he said with a chuckle. "I'm sure I will pay for it later but worth it if I got to come and see you."

"Thank you," I said giving him a big smile turning to snuggle my head into his chest my cheek pressing into the worn leather of his jacket. It was my favorite one to steal when we went riding even though I had my own. "I missed you."

"Missed you too baby," Brantley said then smirked down at me. "Enough that I got my ass on a plane and flew over the ocean."

Brantley's POV

I stirred awake as the daylight filtered in through the windows of Riley's room and smiled down at the beautiful woman curled up sleeping next to me. Well worth the jet lag I was fighting. I gently eased away from her and slipped out of the bed. I looked back at her as she stirred with a sigh, my t-shirt slipping off her shoulder a little as she settled back amongst the covers. Digging in my suitcase, I found what I was looking for then quietly walked back to the bed. I pulled the covers back climbing back in beside Riley turning to my side watching her sleep. Her long hair spread across the pillow, a few strands draped over her face and her hand resting on the pillow. I reached over grabbing my phone snapping a quick photo and loading it up on Instagram and tagging Riley.

@rilesphotosGA She maybe sleeping peacefully. Fingers crossed BGNation that I can get lucky enough for her to say yes when she wakes up. Love of my life right there ya'll.#wishmeluck #prayshedoesn'tkillme

One of the few times I'd actually used the darn thing myself. Usually they kept me away from it because well...I couldn't always keep my mouth shut. I heard Riley's phone chime on the other nightstand as I curled up beside her in the big bed. It kept on buzzing and chiming, and I bit my lip to keep a laugh in as Riley growled in her sleep before her grey eyes blinked open.

"Make it stop," Riley whined burying her head into my chest. I wrapped my arms around her pressing a kiss to her forehead. "Seriously B.....cut it off. Your damn phone is a pain in the ass."

"Baby," I chuckled as she looked up at me. "That's yours."

"Dammit," Riley muttered rolling away from me and snatching her phone up and typing in her code. "Why the hell is my Instagram blowing up at this time of morning? Geez what has Ash tagged me in now." I knew when she finally saw it as her eyes blew out wide and she sat up quickly kicking me in the shin then reached a hand over to smack in the middle of my chest as she dropped her phone. I pushed up to look at her as Riley fumbled for the words. Her eyes welled with tears as I slide my hand over the sheets to lift her left hand up pressing a soft kiss to her knuckles.

"Bbbb..." Riley stuttered looking at me in shock as she looked at her hand then up at me. I grinned over at her. "Are you serious?"

"Depends," I murmured huskily leaning over to hover my lips over hers. "You saying yes?"

Happy Mother's Day

Wishing each and everyone a very Happy Mother's Day!!

Flashback: Your Girl's Home Too: Part I

- -

Late September 2013

Brantley's POV

I killed the engine of my truck in Mama's driveway with a heavy sigh. Out of habit I glanced over to the white house with the black shutters next door searching for a certain blonde to be sitting on the porch swing. I wearily ran a hand over my face then pulled myself out of it. Of course Riley wasn't over there. She was either in Atlanta with her husband or on a photo shoot somewhere. That ship had sailed years ago along with me losing my best friend. Yea, when we were both home we were civil with each other. Couldn't help but be as close as our families were.

I'd been home for Easter earlier this year with Jana tagging along. She'd been determined to finally put a face to a name for Riley. Took all my self control to keep from putting a fist into Jackson's smug face staring me down across the table. Riles had looked as miserable as I had felt at the time. But she hid it well. I had almost been able to confront her over it in the kitchen, but she'd quickly smiled and shrugged me off. Pushing my glasses up on my hat, I made my way into the house finding Mama bustling around in the kitchen. She had her back to the door taking cookies off the pan to cool when I snuck up behind her grabbing her around the waist.

"Ahhh!" Mama yelled then turned her head to see me smiling down at her. She smacked me with a spatula making me yelp. I rubbed my shoulder as she glared at me. "Don't you scare me like that Brantley Keith!"

"Sorry angel," I said with a snicker kissing her cheek as she hugged me tight.

"You look tired baby," Mama muttered rubbing a soft hand on my cheek as I closed my eyes.

"Yes mam," I sighed. "I am. Think we have a chunk of the album wrapped up. And other than an appearance or two and some interviews I am done for a couple of months. Looking forward to getting some hunting done in a few weeks." Mama nodded as she fixed me a glass of tea then watched me closely after handing it to me as I leaned against the counter. I took a sip and raised an eyebrow at her. "What?"

"Your girl's home too," she said quietly studying my reaction. I knew exactly who she was talking about, I just didn't want to have this conversation right now. "Came blazing in to town a few days ago."

"Don't have a girl Mama," I muttered taking another sip and not looking at her. I jerked when I felt a sharp tug on my ear.

"You know who I mean," Mama grumbled rolling her eyes.

"Mama," I growled quietly. "She hasn't been mine for a long time. Made that abundantly clear with that rock on her finger and a new last name."

"Well....." she drawled as I felt my phone vibrate in my pocket. "I know for a fact that rock is missing from a certain finger."

"Don't play with me angel," I said biting my lip and tugged my phone out of my pocket.

Ash: Hey, heard through the grapevine you were in. You busy this evening?

BG: I've barely been home and you heard it through the grapevine??? No, I am not busy if Cam wants to hang out.

Ash: Finnneee.... My grapevine consists of my husband and your brother. They are reliable sources. Actually I had a favor to ask. I have someone who's around that would like to see you. Please B, for old times sake. Time to put the past to bed.

I glanced up at Mama who was giving me a knowing look then looked back at my phone for a minute debating how to answer. Yes, I would like to see her. If I was honest with myself, I missed my best friend. Other than a once in the blue moon text, we really hadn't talked much the last few years.

BG: Are you shitting me Ash? Cause I will tell you right now, if you are playing with me, that shit isn't funny at all.

Ash: Not shitting you B! And don't take that tone with me mister! Five sound good for you?

BG: Fine. I'll be over there in a little bit.

Ash: Good. She really wants to see you B. So dammit, you better be good!

I rolled my eyes and jerked when Mama smacked me upside the head as she read my text.

BG: I'm always good Ash. Practically a saint.

Ash: More like a monk here lately.

BG: Whatever Ash. I told you, I was through with running through women. Being sober does that you know.

Ash: Thank God you got rid of the SheDevil!

BG: Kiss my ass! You know why and I am better off!

I slipped my phone into my pocket and turned wrapping my arms around Mama. I glanced at the clock knowing I didn't have long before I needed to be at Ashley's. Damn woman, knew how to time it just right so I didn't over think it. I heard my phone go off again as Mama kissed my cheek and pulled it out. My eyes widened at the message.

Ash: She left him BG. Just thought you should know that beforehand.

I felt like my heart was about to pound out of my chest at the words wondering if they were real or not. I blinked and read them again. Mama laid a hand on my arm jerking my attention to her.

"Ashley told you she left," she murmured. "Didn't she?"

"Yes mam," I managed to croak out as my chest tightened.

"Go on son," Mama said giving me an encouraging smile. "Won't hurt to take a ride for old times' sake."

"Mama," I whispered sliding my phone in my pocket and looking down at my feet. "I don't know if I can...." I licked my lips searching for the words. "I mean I'm not sure if she can ever forgive me. Because I don't know if I can forgive myself. We've been distant the last few years."

"Got to start somewhere baby," she said with a quiet sigh before standing on her tip toes to kiss my cheek then shoving me to the door. "Go on. I didn't raise a chicken. Last I checked I raised a hellraiser."

I rolled my eyes at her and ducked out the door before she could smack me. I climbed in and pointed my truck towards my destination my hands gripping the wheel so hard my knuckles where white underneath my rings. They started to sweat as I turned into Ashley and Eli's gravel drive. I took a deep breath before killing the truck and climbed out praying my shaky knees didn't give out on me. I mean we had seen each other, but other than a polite hello here and there we hadn't said too much to each other.

The creak of the screen door pulled me from my nervous thoughts as I lifted my head up. I paused halfway to the wooden porch dead in my tracks as I saw Riley standing there. In a pair of cutoff shorts, a faded UGA t-shirt biting her lip. The sleek bob her honey blonde hair was cut into made me ache for the high ponytail that she used to wear. I locked eyes with her grey ones losing my breath. I swallowed deeply as she nervously shuffled her feet back and forth unsure of what to do. Ashley appeared behind her a second later giving her a playful shove off the porch. She gave me a bright smile and a wave.

"Have fun kids!!" Ashley called out with a laugh as Riley stumbled down the steps. She waved us both away as she looked back over her shoulder. "Now get out of here before Tinsley realizes Unca B is around too and demands your attention!"

I shook my head with a snicker as she darted back in the house. She was right. My goddaughter would demand my undivided attention if she knew I was here. Had been a little busy lately. I looked at Riley who had paused giving me a tentative smile. Unable to help myself, I opened my arms and grinned as she took of running and jumped letting me catch her. I boosted her up so she could wrap her legs around me and held her tight as she gripped the back of my neck like she would never let go. Peace, that is what I immediately felt as she snuggled closer. I took a deep breath of her familiar sugary vanilla scent that mad my mouth water for a taste. Riley sighed against my neck.

"God, I have missed you Riles," I murmured against the softness of her hair. "I'm so damn sorry."

Riley pulled back lifting her head to look at me with a shy smile as she unlocked her legs and giggled when she realized her feet were still dangling over the driveway from me holding her up.

"Water under the bridge B," her soft voice mumbled as she placed a hand on my bearded cheek. I noticed a light sheen of tears in her eyes before she blinked them away. I slowly lowered her to her feet then laced my fingers with hers and backed up to my truck. "Want to get out of here?"

"Yes mam. I know just the place," I said with a wink opening the door and flipping the console up so she could slide over. Riley scrambled in sliding over to the passenger side then lowered the console as I climbed in. I started the truck then looked over at her sitting in the passenger side seat like she had always been there. Just like she was always meant to be. "This really happening?

"Yes," Riley said with a quiet laugh shoving my shoulder with a smile as I pointed the truck out of town. I smiled back at her as she turned to look out the window. She grew quiet as she idly tapped her finger along with the radio on the console. I couldn't help but notice the bare ring finger on her left hand. The only indication was the pale circle on her tan skin. I laid my hand over hers making Riley look over at me.

"You okay Riles," I asked quietly as I squeezed her hand gently. She looked down at my hand then back up shrugging her shoulders.

"Riles....." she murmured as sad smile turning up her full pink lips. I was surprised at the need I felt to lean over and gently kiss them. "Been a long time since I have heard that, and I forgot how much I missed it. I had to get out of Atlanta for a little bit before my next assignment. Coming home seemed like the best thing to do."

How Forever Feels

R iley's POV

Feeling the bed shift behind me, a smile curved on my face as a warm pair of lips brushed my bare shoulder. I snuggled back further into the warmth holding me feeling myself drift off again. I knew I was going to have a pounding headache as soon as I was fully awake. It may or may not have been a pajama and wine night for me and Ashley. A quiet chuckle coupled with the tickle of a beard along my neck made me crack an eye open.

"Five more minutes," I grunted trying to put my pillow over my head. "Just five more minutes. PLeeeasseeee...."

"What do you I get?" Brantley whispered darkly in my ear causing a delicious shiver to trail down my spine. "I think there was a lot of promises that someone made last night while they were out having girl's night with Ashley. Something about your mouth and my......"

"Can I I.O.U. babe?" I asked weakly as I shifted to bury my head in his warm neck. I closed my eyes with a sigh. A hand slid down squeezing my ass through the pajama pants I was wearing making me sigh. Brantley pulled me closer wrapping my body around his with a quiet laugh.

"Wow Riles...." he said with a quiet pout lifting my left hand up to brush his lips over my wedding band. That's when it hit my foggy brain. A long finger tapped the end of my nose as I blushed sheepishly. "Ahhh there it is. Someone finally...."

"Happy Anniversary baby," I said softly. Wrapping my arms around his neck I pulled his lips down to mine quickly getting lost in a kiss that made my toes curls. Five years. It was hard to believe it had been five years since I had finally had my dream of marrying my best friend come true. Two weeks to the day after he had proposed to me in Ireland. When I had looked at his schedule and mine on the flight home, I had thought he would fall out of his chair in shock when I pointed at the date. Once he realized I was serious he had been all for it. It had been just us, both our Mama's, and Kolby to give me away.

Dialed down big time from the full-blown Southern affair Jackson's mother had insisted we have. No huge puffy one of a kind concoction. My dress has been so simple, barefoot with flowers in my hair. We'd gotten married under our tree with tears in both of our eyes. Every day I thanked the good Lord for keeping this man in my life all these years. I never doubted that he loved me unconditionally. Was life perfect? Hell no. We were both too stubborn and hard headed to see eye to eye at times. No matter how mad we got at one another, I never doubted that he loved me.

A warm hand sliding under my t-shirt made a moan slip out as I arched my back pressing my hard nipple into Brantley's hand. Wrapping my legs around his waist, I pulled him closer rubbing against him. I slid a hand down his chest to tug at the waistband of his sweatpants when I heard the pounding of two sets of feet. Brantley broke the kiss dropping his head down to my shoulder with a groan as I tried to recover my senses. We had about five seconds before that door swung open.

"Little cock blockers," Brantley growled into my skin making me giggle. I smacked his shoulder pushing him to roll off me with a sigh. He glared at me for laughing. "Stop laughing Riles. I am serious. I've only been home two days and a quickie before car pick up at school has been it. You've been at your studio, out with Ashley last night."

"Welcome to parenthood B," I said with a snicker grabbing the end of his beard pulling his lips down to mine. "For one they missed you. Two...I may have bribed Kolby to babysit tonight so it will just be me and you in this big old house all alone. Whatever will we do?"

"I'll tell you what we are gonna do," he said with a dark smirk leaning over me to whisper in my ear. "I am gonna fuck you to you cum so hard you see stars. You will cum again and again until I decide we are done. So sweetheart, it's going to be a very, very long night."

"Shit...." I whimpered closing my eyes as his words sent shocks through my veins. "Baby, if I even had underwear on they would be soaked. So not fair. Think I can bribe Kolby to take them early."

"Don't tell me shit like that Riles and I can't do anything about it," Brantley growled glaring down at me as I batted my eyes at him. A series of quiet knocks sounded on our door. At least we had broken the habit of them barging in....somewhat. Eyes narrowed at me one more time. "Your ass will pay for that later baby. Mark my words. Come in!"

"Promises, promises," I chuckled kissing him quickly as we both sat up leaning against our wooden headboard. The door barged open and thundering feet sounded before the bed bounced followed by giggles. I still remember the look of shock then joy on Brantley's face about a week after we had gotten married. Thinking I had caught the flu from one of my clients, I had gone to the doctor. When she had come back in telling me I was pregnant, I had immediately burst into tears. Unable to wait, I had Face Timed Brantley from the office interrupting soundcheck.

The boys still hadn't let him live down the fact PJ had needed to catch him before he hit the stage face first. That was just the first of surprise we had I smiled at the sight of our four-year old twins trying their best to talk over one another to tell their dad what he had missed while he had been on the road. They'd stayed with my mama last night while we had a night out separately with Eli and Ashley. Bryce and Brianna were equal parts of each of us. Long of the short of it was...they were hell on wheels most days.

"Daddy..." Bri said snapping her fingers making Bryce narrow his eyes looking so much like Brantley I couldn't help but laugh. He reached over tugging one of her blonde pigtails earning him a growl from his sister. Her identical green eyes glowed with her temper. Ten minutes older and he thought he was the complete boss of her. Most days she showed him different. I had no idea where they got it from.

"Bryce don't pull your sister's hair little man," Brantley said with a chuckle. "Did y'all have fun with Nana?"

"We did!" Bryce said his eyes lighting up. That's when I noticed the chocolate smudges around his lips. "She let us have the chocolate chip cookies we made last night for breakfast." He hung his head a little. "Sorry Daddy, we forgot to save some."

"It's alright buddy," Brantley grinned. "I'll just have to get Mama to make me some. Bet if we offer to help her she might."

"Last time y'all did, I was scrubbing cookie dough for days," I said dryly pursing my lips at my husband. "Someone had to start a food fight."

"But Mama...." Bri drawled sighing dramatically. "Daddy said by the time we were done you looked good enough to eat."

"That she did Princess...that she did," Brantley said wiggling his eyebrows at me. I smacked his shoulder making the kids laugh. They launched into a story about something they had done in school the previous day making me smile even when they paused mid-sentence to argue with each other. Meeting my eyes over their heads, Brantley gave me a heart stopping smile. It had felt like we took a crazy train to get our lives where we are now. But the most important thing of all was that we had come out on the other side together. We'd proved goodbye never meant a thing when it came to us. We had always been meant to be. Even with all the heartbreak, I wouldn't change the life we have now. I thank God each day for my husband and our children.

THE END

Authors note: Thank y'all so much for reading this one and I hope you enjoyed them!